My dear Rose,

The planet of Ludokaa was full of surprises, including the most astonishing sunset I have ever seen!

Unfortunately, the sunset was so enchanting that the planet's inhabitants fought for the privilege of viewing it. I'm happy to say that they were able to set aside their differences and learn to enjoy the wonders of their planet together.

It is a rare privilege to share with others the feelings produced by such beauty. In fact, sharing a beautiful thing with others makes it even more beautiful.

If only the Snake could learn this lesson!

The Little Prince

First American edition published in 2014 by Graphic Universe™.

Le Petit Prince ™

based on the masterpiece by Antoine de Saint-Exupéry

© 2014 LPPM
An animated series based on the novel *Le Petit Prince* by Antoine de Saint-Exupéry
Developed for television by Matthieu Delaporte, Alexandre de la Patellière, and Bertrand Gatignol
Directed by Pierre-Alain Chartier

© 2014 ÉDITIONS GLÉNAT
Copyright © 2014 by Lerner Publishing Group, Inc., for the current edition

Graphic Universe™
A division of Lerner Publishing Group, Inc.
241 First Avenue North
Minneapolis, MN 55401 U.S.A.

Website address: www.lernerbooks.com

Library of Congress Cataloging-in-Publication Data

Bruneau, Clotilde.
 [Planète des Lacrimavoras. English]
 The Planet of Tear-eaters / story by Delphine Dubos ; design and illustrations by Elyum Studio ; adaptation by Clotilde Bruneau ; translation, Anne Collins Smith and Owen Smith. — 1st American ed.
  p. cm. — (The little prince ; #13)
  ISBN 978—0—7613—8763—3 (lib. bdg. : alk. paper)
  ISBN 978—1—4677—2423—4 (eBook)
  1. Graphic novels. I. Dubos, Delphine. II Smith, Anne Collins. III. Smith, Owen. IV. Elyum Studio.
 V. Petit Prince (Television program) VI. Title.
 PZ7.7.B8Pm 2014
 741.5'944—dc23   2013014075

Manufactured in the United States of America
1 — PC — 12/31/13

THE NEW ADVENTURES
BASED ON THE MASTERPIECE BY ANTOINE DE SAINT-EXUPÉRY

The Little Prince

THE PLANET OF TEAR-EATERS

Based on the animated series and an original story by Delphine Dubos

Design: Elyum Studio
Story: Clotilde Bruneau
Artistic Direction: Didier Poli
Art: Diane Fayolle
Backgrounds: Isa Python
Coloring: Moonsun
Editing: Christine Chatal
Editorial Consultant: Didier Convard

Translation: Anne and Owen Smith

Graphic Universe™ • Minneapolis

THE LITTLE PRINCE

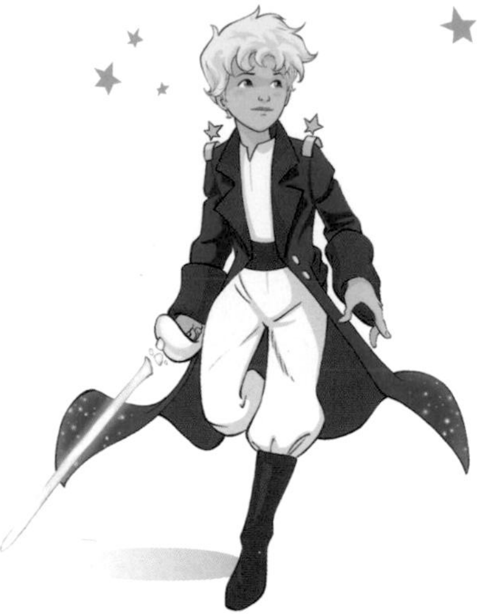

The Little Prince has extraordinary gifts. His sense of wonder allows him to discover what no one else can see. The Little Prince can communicate with all the beings in the universe, even the animals and plants. His powers grow over the course of his adventures.

The Prince's uniform:
When he transforms into the uniform of a prince, he is more agile and quick. When faced with difficult situations, the Little Prince also uses a sword that lets him sketch and bring to life anything from his imagination.

His sketchbook:
When he is not in his Prince's clothing, the Little Prince carries a sketchbook. When he blows on the pages, they take wing and form objects that he'll find very useful. Like his sword, it's powered by stardust collected on his travels.

FOX

A grouch, a trickster, and, so he says, interested only in his next meal, Fox is in reality the Little Prince's best friend. As such, he is always there to give him help but also just as much to help him to grow and to learn about the world.

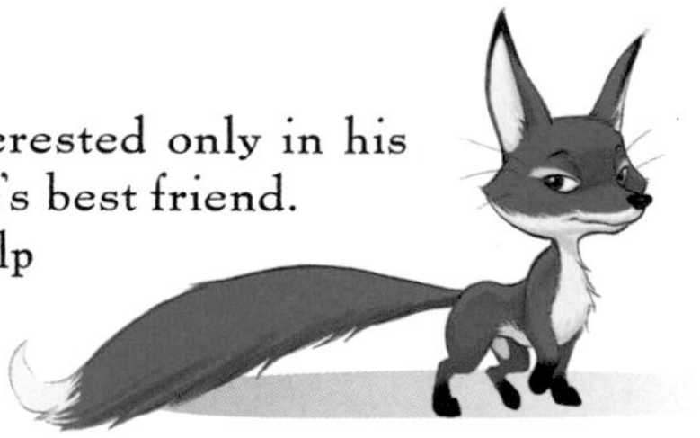

THE SNAKE

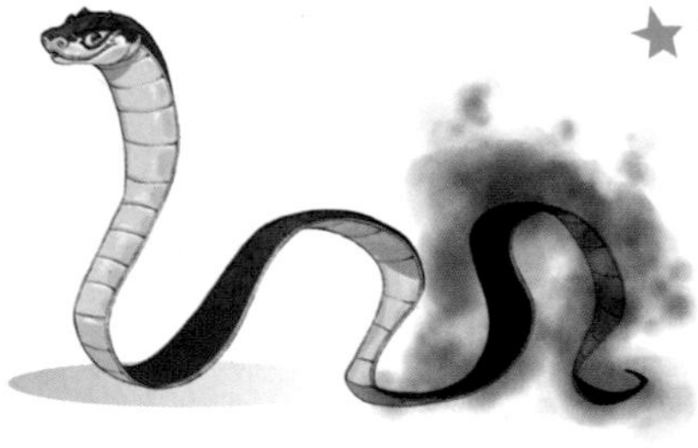

Even though the Little Prince still does not know exactly why, there can be no doubt that the Snake has set his mind to plunging the entire universe into darkness! And to accomplish his goal, this malicious being is ready to use any form of deception. However, the Snake never takes action himself. He prefers to bring out the wickedness in those beings he has chosen to bite, tempting them to put their own worlds in danger.

THE GLOOMIES

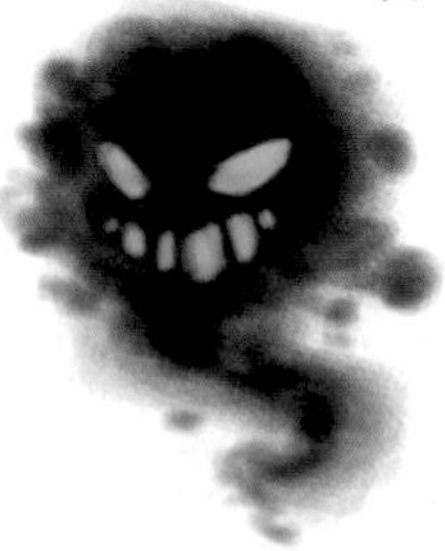

When people who have been "bitten" by the Snake have completely destroyed their own planets, they become Gloomies, slaves to their Snake master. The Gloomies act as a group and carry out the Snake's most vile orders so he can get the better of the Little Prince!

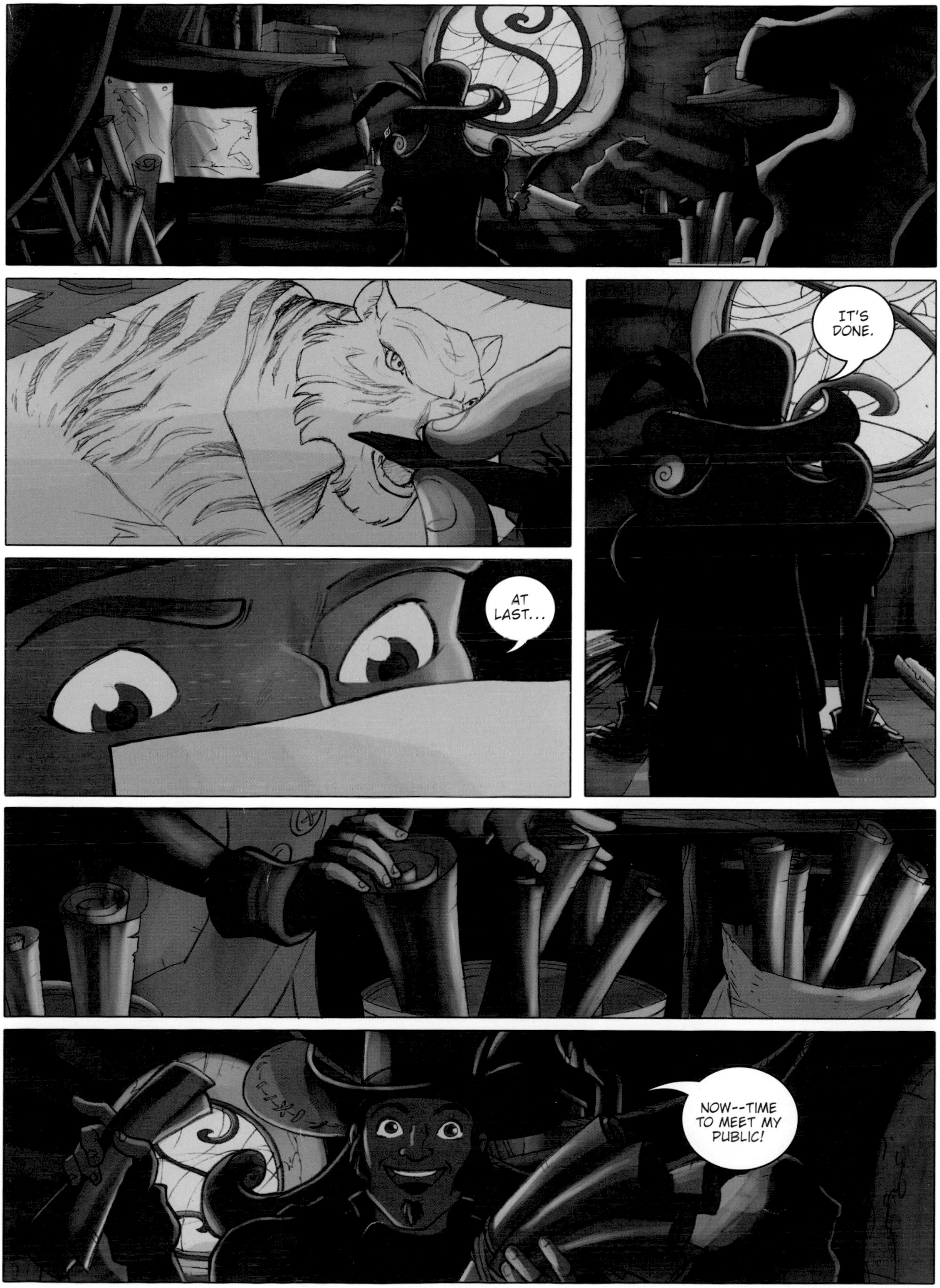
IT'S DONE.
AT LAST...
NOW--TIME TO MEET MY PUBLIC!

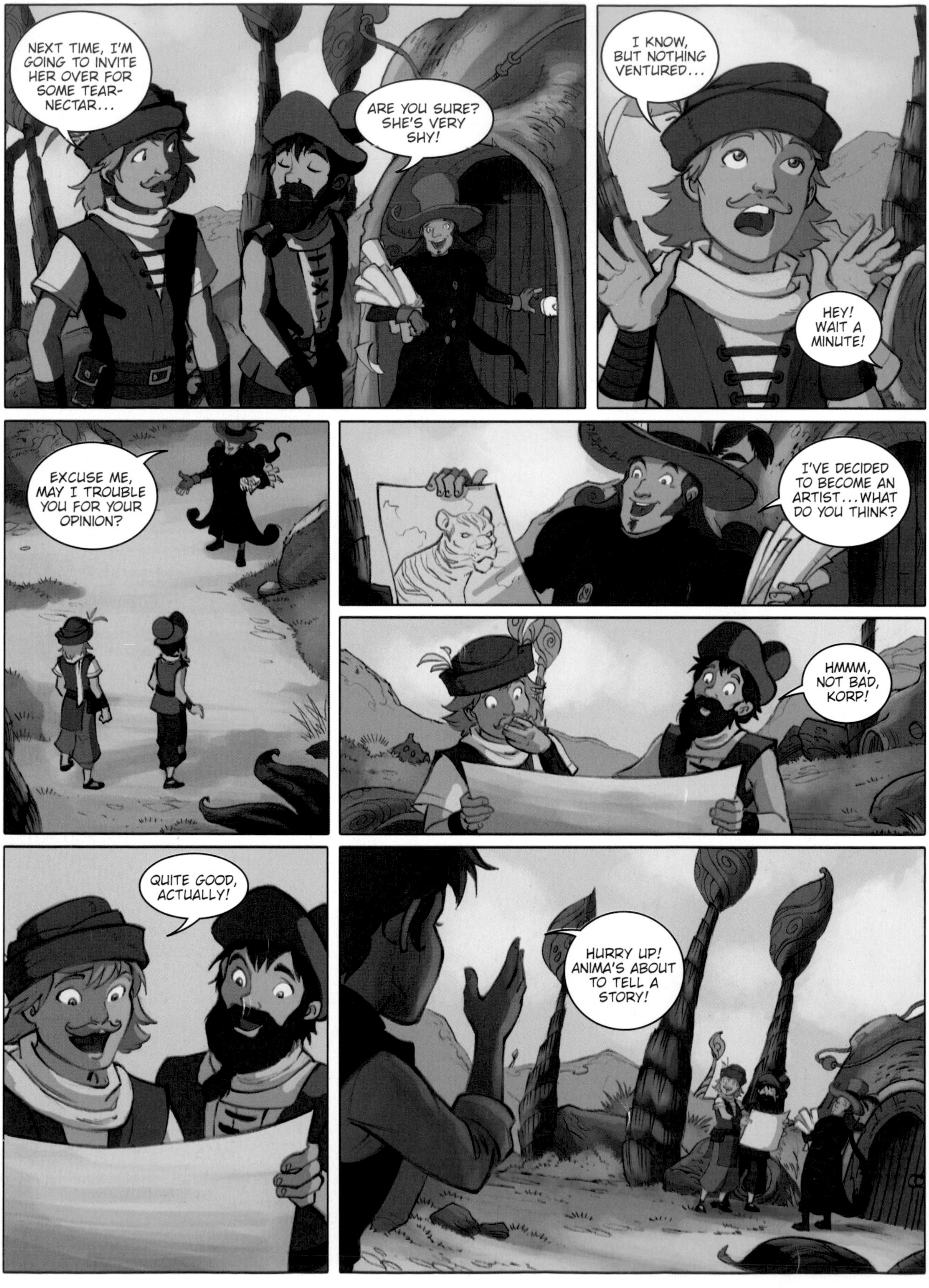
NEXT TIME, I'M GOING TO INVITE HER OVER FOR SOME TEAR-NECTAR...
ARE YOU SURE? SHE'S VERY SHY!
I KNOW, BUT NOTHING VENTURED...
HEY! WAIT A MINUTE!
EXCUSE ME, MAY I TROUBLE YOU FOR YOUR OPINION?
I'VE DECIDED TO BECOME AN ARTIST...WHAT DO YOU THINK?
HMMM, NOT BAD, KORP!
QUITE GOOD, ACTUALLY!
HURRY UP! ANIMA'S ABOUT TO TELL A STORY!

THE NEW FABULIST? SHE'S FANTASTIC!
NOT TO MENTION BEAUTIFUL!
I WONDER WHAT TODAY'S STORY WILL BE...
I HOPE THERE'S A TIGER IN IT!
I'M SURE THERE WILL BE PLENTY OF EMO-BUBBLES!
HEY... WAIT!
...

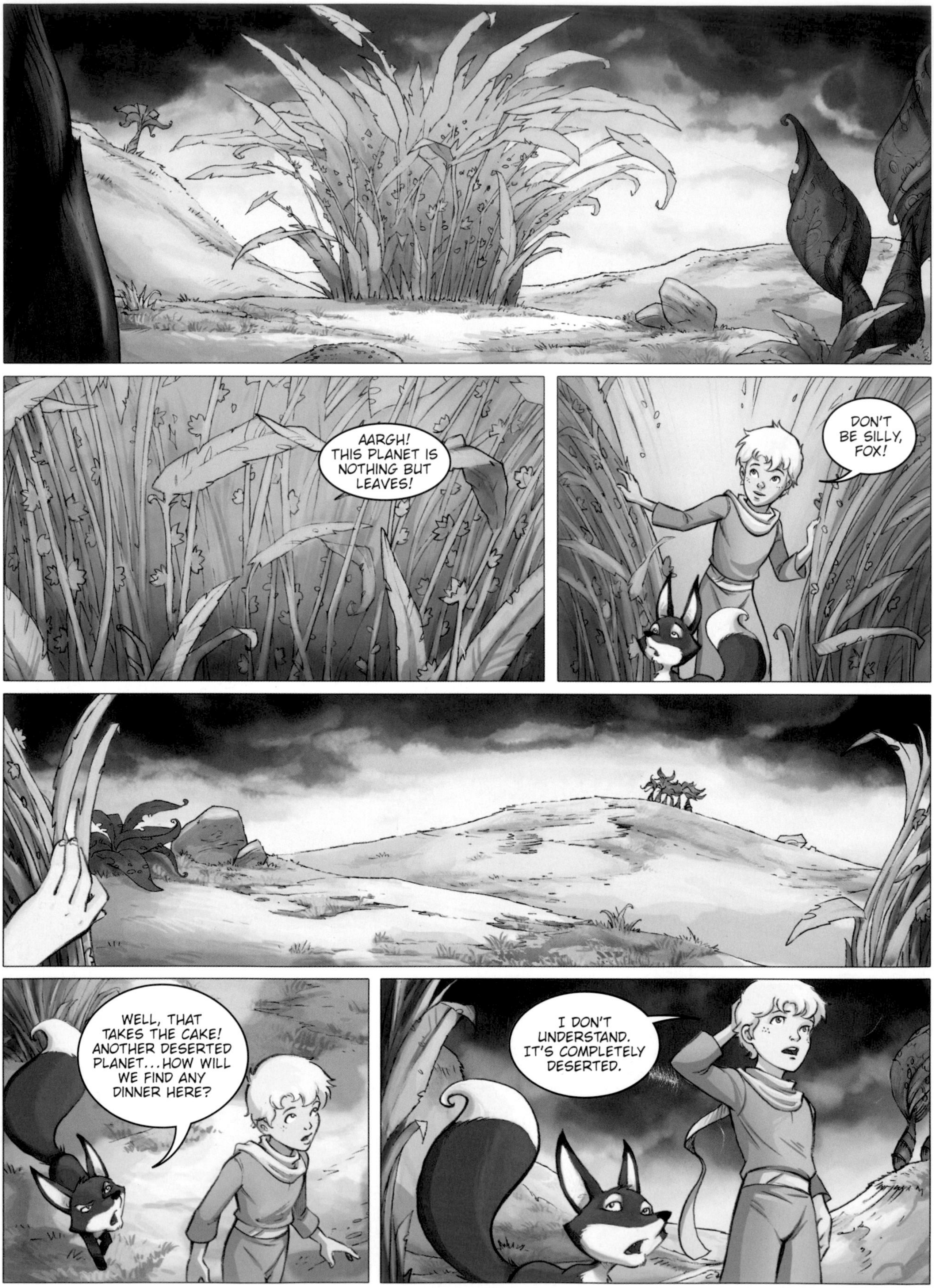
AARGH! THIS PLANET IS NOTHING BUT LEAVES!
DON'T BE SILLY, FOX!
WELL, THAT TAKES THE CAKE! ANOTHER DESERTED PLANET... HOW WILL WE FIND ANY DINNER HERE?
I DON'T UNDERSTAND. IT'S COMPLETELY DESERTED.

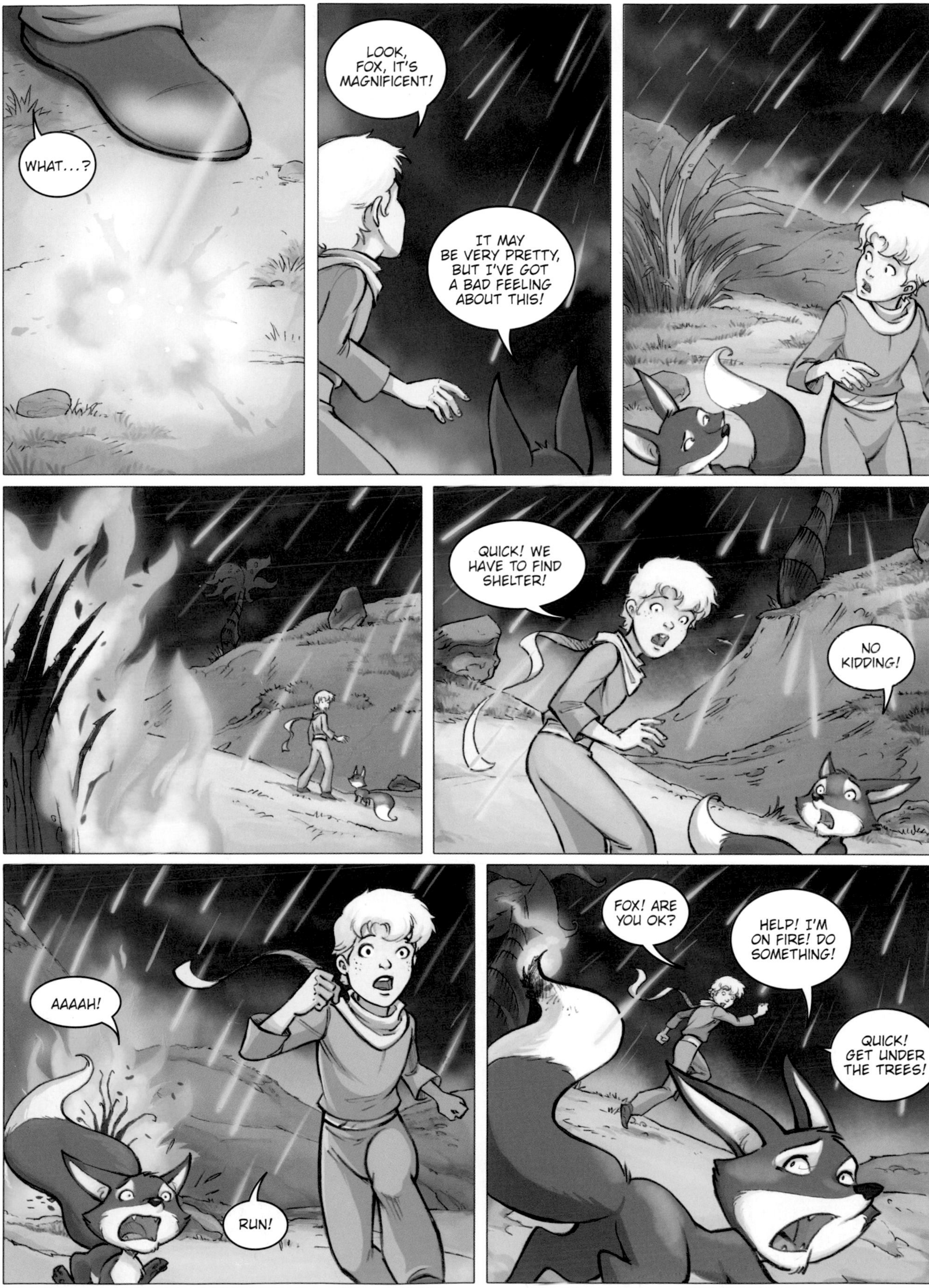
WHAT...?
LOOK, FOX, IT'S MAGNIFICENT!
IT MAY BE VERY PRETTY, BUT I'VE GOT A BAD FEELING ABOUT THIS!
QUICK! WE HAVE TO FIND SHELTER!
NO KIDDING!
AAAAH!
RUN!
FOX! ARE YOU OK?
HELP! I'M ON FIRE! DO SOMETHING!
QUICK! GET UNDER THE TREES!

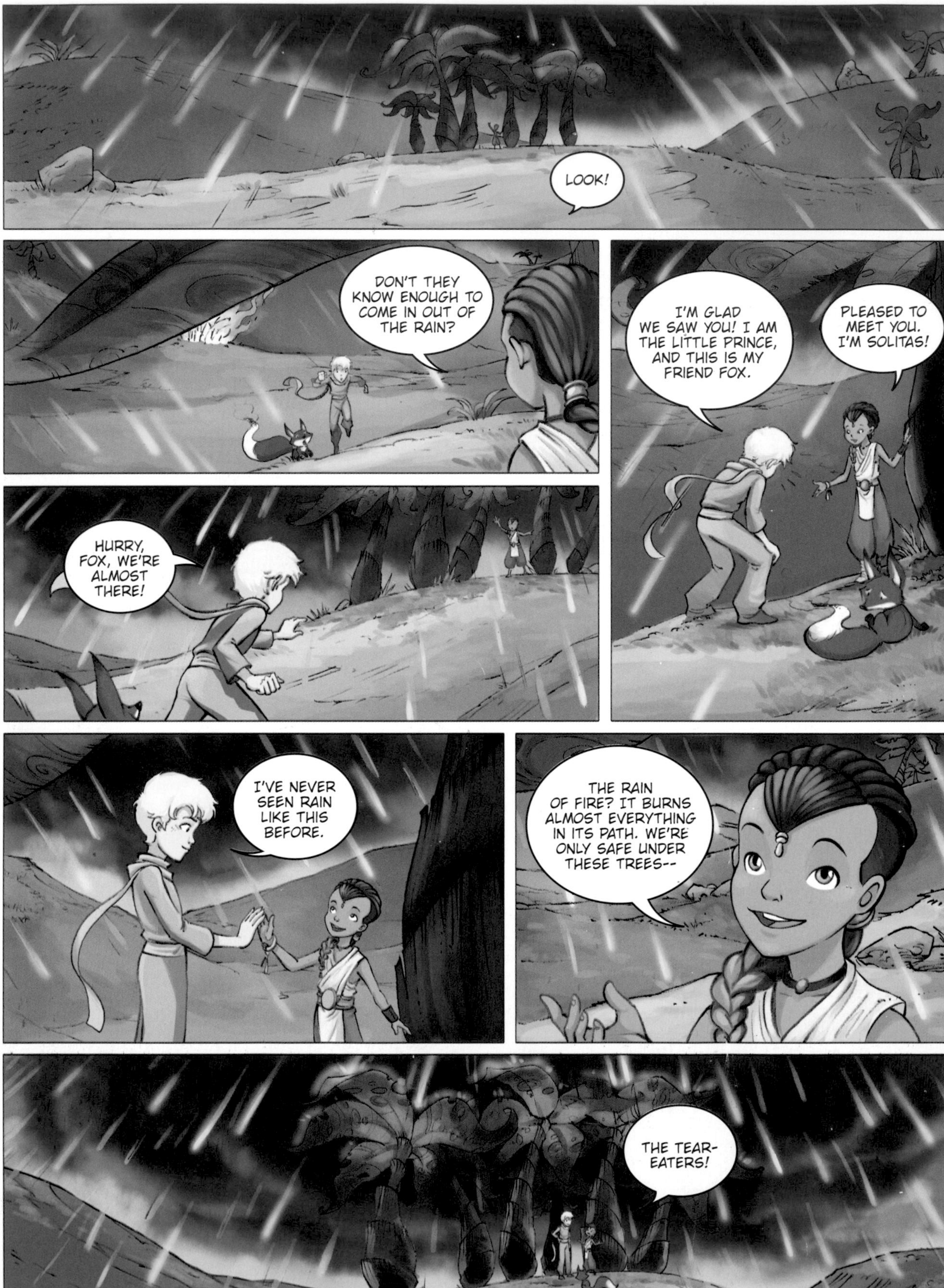
LOOK!
DON'T THEY KNOW ENOUGH TO COME IN OUT OF THE RAIN?
I'M GLAD WE SAW YOU! I AM THE LITTLE PRINCE, AND THIS IS MY FRIEND FOX.
PLEASED TO MEET YOU. I'M SOLITAS!
HURRY, FOX, WE'RE ALMOST THERE!
I'VE NEVER SEEN RAIN LIKE THIS BEFORE.
THE RAIN OF FIRE? IT BURNS ALMOST EVERYTHING IN ITS PATH. WE'RE ONLY SAFE UNDER THESE TREES--
THE TEAR-EATERS!

THE RAIN FALLS ONCE A DAY... FORTUNATELY, THE PLANET HAS PLENTY OF TEAR-EATERS TO SHELTER OUR PEOPLE.

BUT HOW DO THE TREES SURVIVE WITHOUT RAIN? I MEAN, WITHOUT RAINWATER?

WHY, THEY DRINK EMO-BUBBLES, OF COURSE!

EMO-WHAT? ARE YOU JUST MAKING THIS UP?

WE'VE NEVER HEARD THOSE WORDS BEFORE!

HUH?

NO! WHEN THE FABULIST TELLS HER STORY, THE FABULEMES CAUSE THE LISTENERS TO PRODUCE EMO-BUBBLES! THEN THE EMO-BUBBLES NOURISH THE TEAR-EATERS!

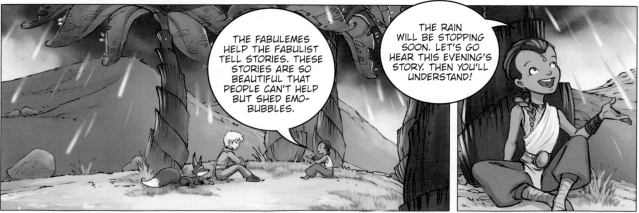

THE FABULEMES HELP THE FABULIST TELL STORIES. THESE STORIES ARE SO BEAUTIFUL THAT PEOPLE CAN'T HELP BUT SHED EMO-BUBBLES.

THE RAIN WILL BE STOPPING SOON. LET'S GO HEAR THIS EVENING'S STORY. THEN YOU'LL UNDERSTAND!

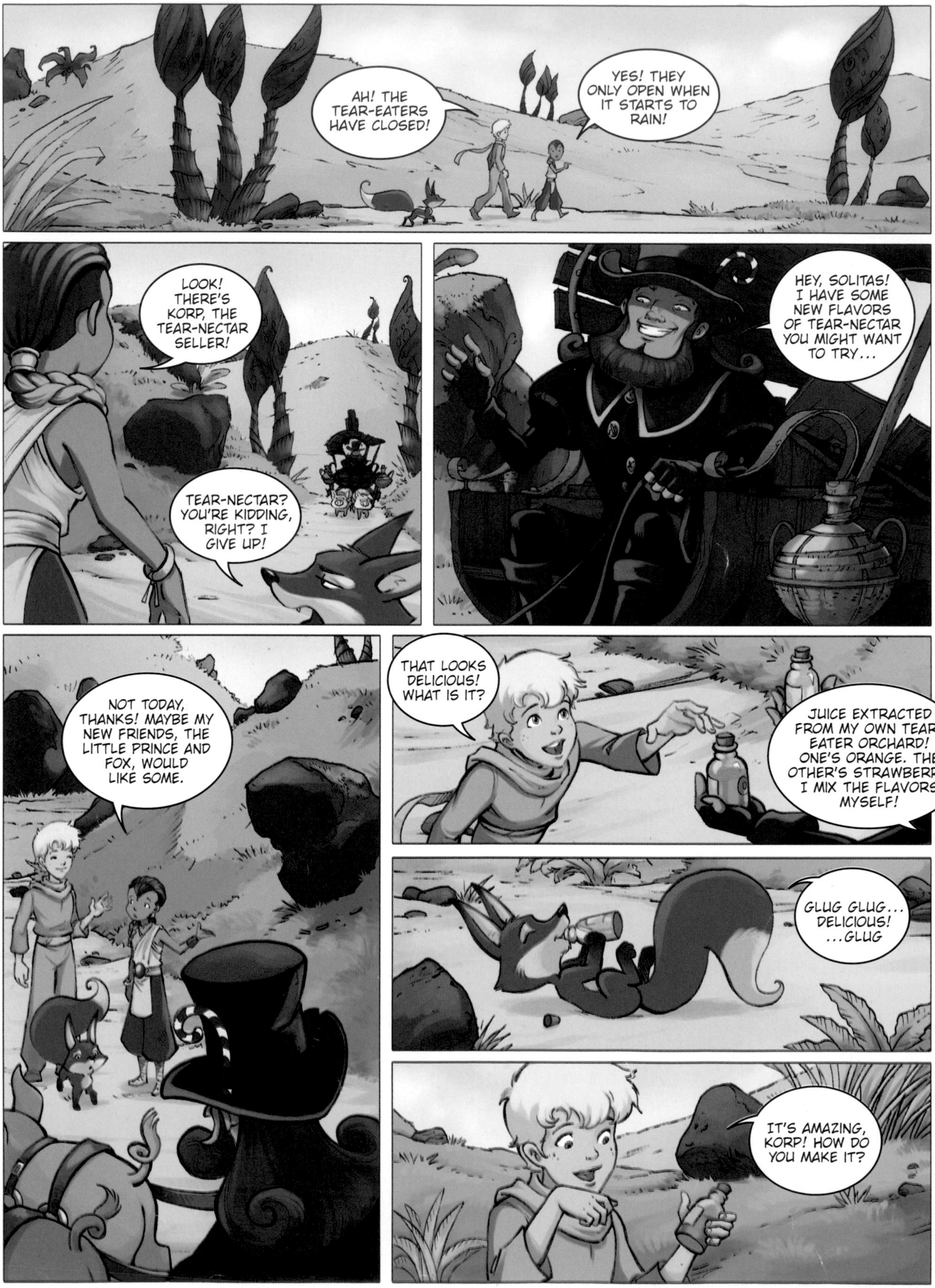
AH! THE TEAR-EATERS HAVE CLOSED!
YES! THEY ONLY OPEN WHEN IT STARTS TO RAIN!
LOOK! THERE'S KORP, THE TEAR-NECTAR SELLER!
TEAR-NECTAR? YOU'RE KIDDING, RIGHT? I GIVE UP!
HEY, SOLITAS! I HAVE SOME NEW FLAVORS OF TEAR-NECTAR YOU MIGHT WANT TO TRY...
NOT TODAY, THANKS! MAYBE MY NEW FRIENDS, THE LITTLE PRINCE AND FOX, WOULD LIKE SOME.
THAT LOOKS DELICIOUS! WHAT IS IT?
JUICE EXTRACTED FROM MY OWN TEAR-EATER ORCHARD! ONE'S ORANGE. THE OTHER'S STRAWBERRY. I MIX THE FLAVORS MYSELF!
GLUG GLUG... DELICIOUS! ...GLUG
IT'S AMAZING, KORP! HOW DO YOU MAKE IT?

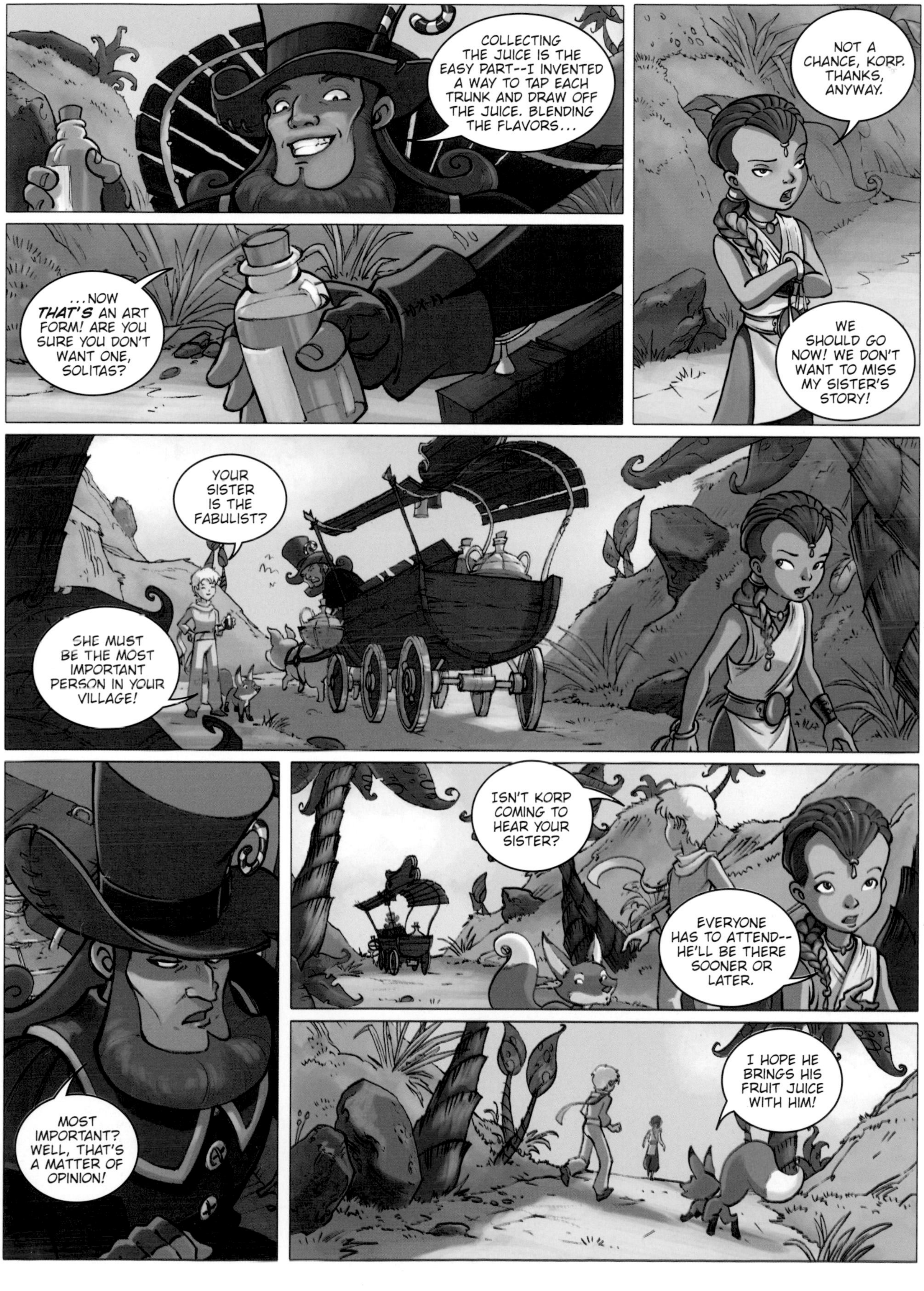
COLLECTING THE JUICE IS THE EASY PART--I INVENTED A WAY TO TAP EACH TRUNK AND DRAW OFF THE JUICE. BLENDING THE FLAVORS...
...NOW *THAT'S* AN ART FORM! ARE YOU SURE YOU DON'T WANT ONE, SOLITAS?
NOT A CHANCE, KORP. THANKS, ANYWAY.
WE SHOULD GO NOW! WE DON'T WANT TO MISS MY SISTER'S STORY!
YOUR SISTER IS THE FABULIST?
SHE MUST BE THE MOST IMPORTANT PERSON IN YOUR VILLAGE!
MOST IMPORTANT? WELL, THAT'S A MATTER OF OPINION!
ISN'T KORP COMING TO HEAR YOUR SISTER?
EVERYONE HAS TO ATTEND--HE'LL BE THERE SOONER OR LATER.
I HOPE HE BRINGS HIS FRUIT JUICE WITH HIM!

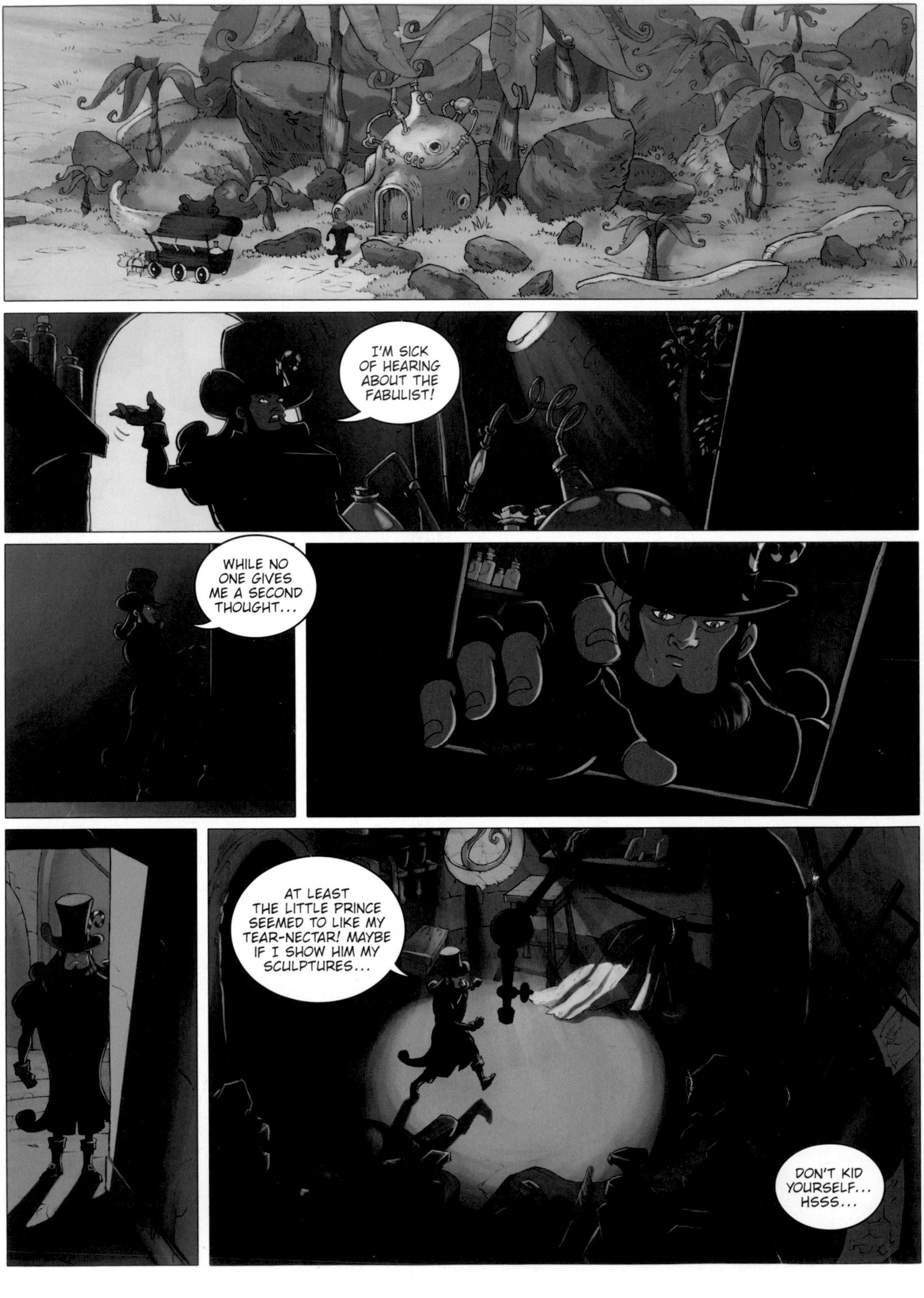
I'M SICK OF HEARING ABOUT THE FABULIST!
WHILE NO ONE GIVES ME A SECOND THOUGHT...
AT LEAST THE LITTLE PRINCE SEEMED TO LIKE MY TEAR-NECTAR! MAYBE IF I SHOW HIM MY SCULPTURES...
DON'T KID YOURSELF... HSSS...

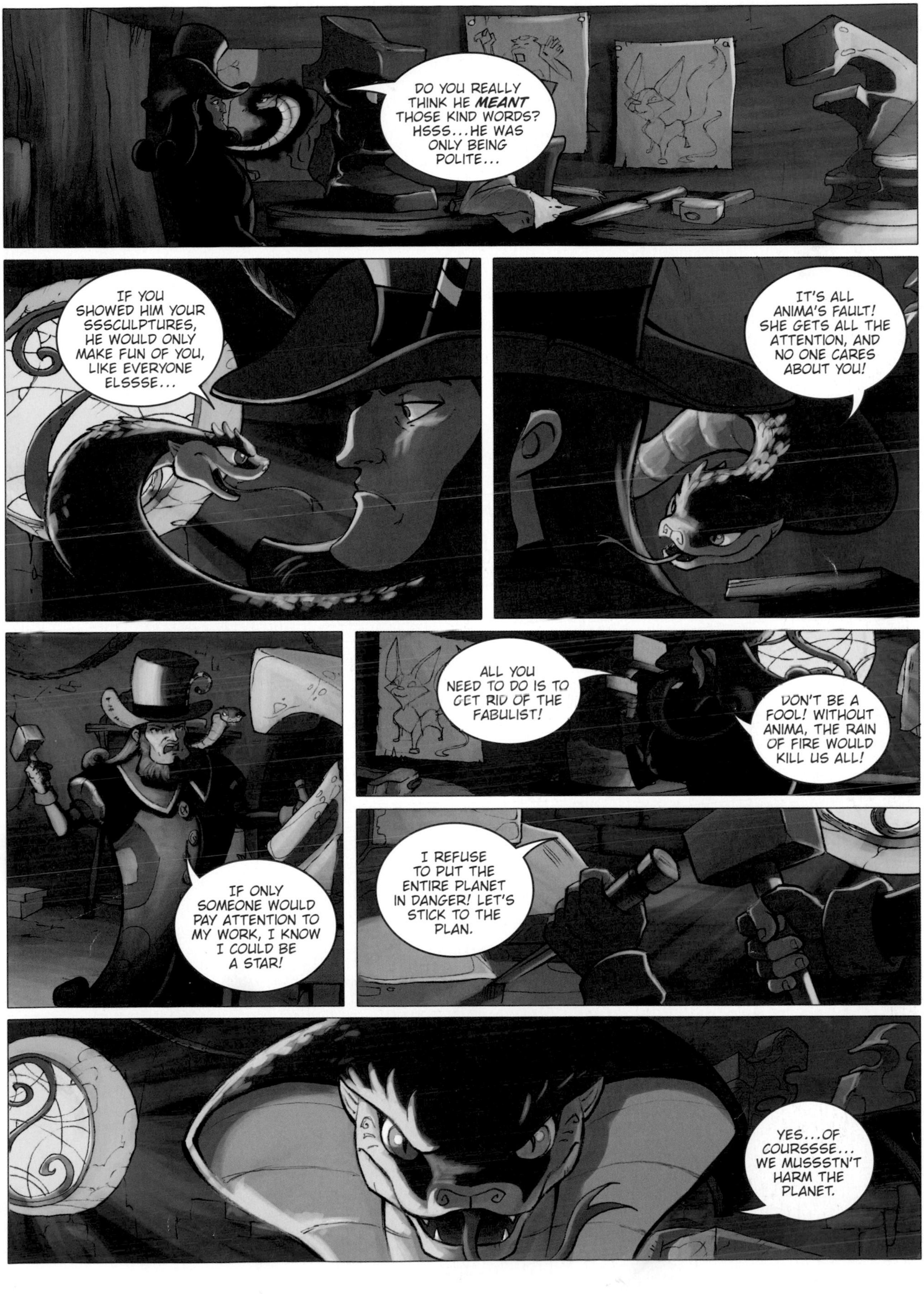
DO YOU REALLY THINK HE **MEANT** THOSE KIND WORDS? HSSS...HE WAS ONLY BEING POLITE...
IF YOU SHOWED HIM YOUR SSSCULPTURES, HE WOULD ONLY MAKE FUN OF YOU, LIKE EVERYONE ELSSSE...
IT'S ALL ANIMA'S FAULT! SHE GETS ALL THE ATTENTION, AND NO ONE CARES ABOUT YOU!
IF ONLY SOMEONE WOULD PAY ATTENTION TO MY WORK, I KNOW I COULD BE A STAR!
ALL YOU NEED TO DO IS TO GET RID OF THE FABULIST!
DON'T BE A FOOL! WITHOUT ANIMA, THE RAIN OF FIRE WOULD KILL US ALL!
I REFUSE TO PUT THE ENTIRE PLANET IN DANGER! LET'S STICK TO THE PLAN.
YES...OF COURSSSE... WE MUSSSTN'T HARM THE PLANET.

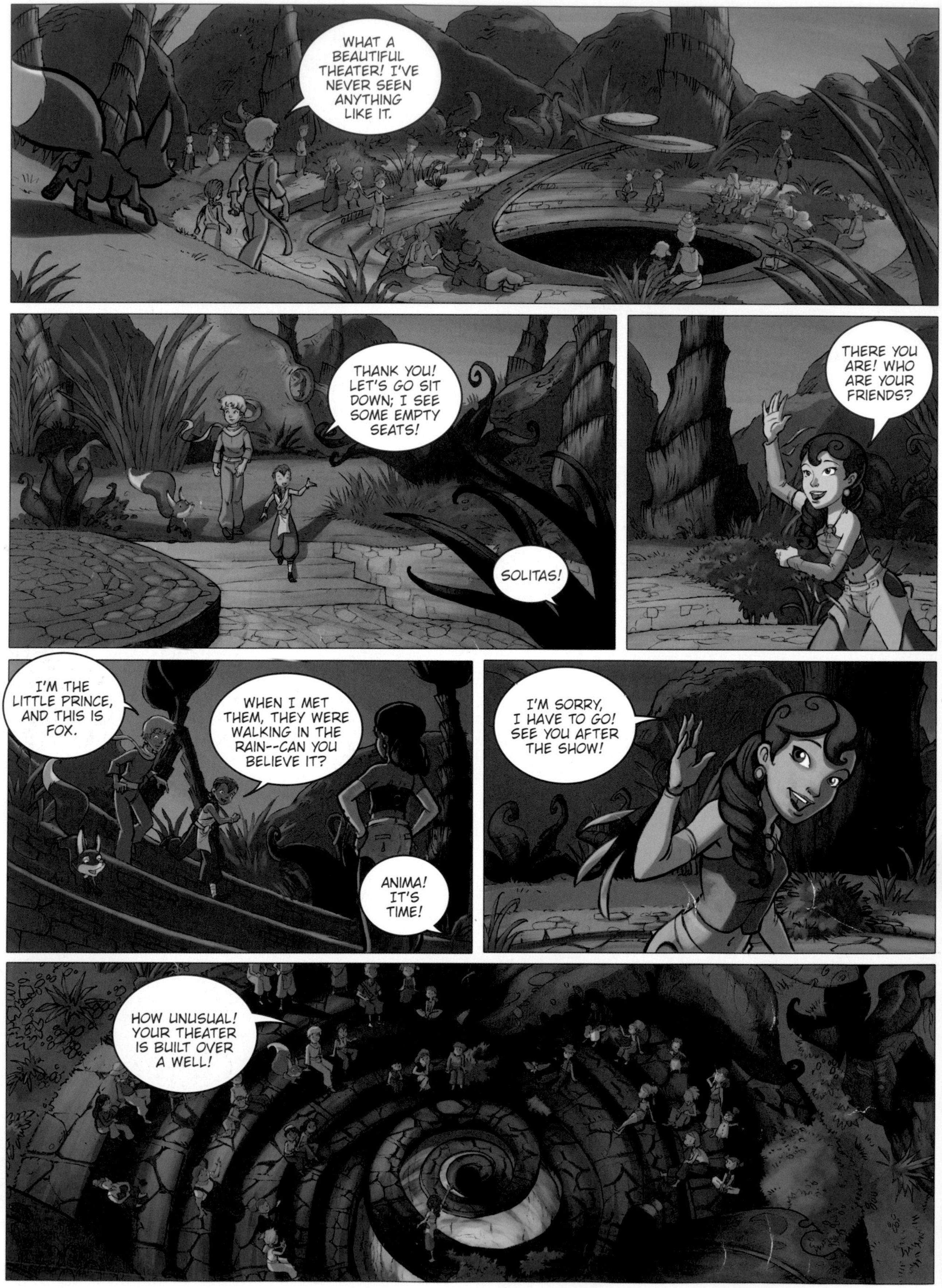
WHAT A BEAUTIFUL THEATER! I'VE NEVER SEEN ANYTHING LIKE IT.
THANK YOU! LET'S GO SIT DOWN; I SEE SOME EMPTY SEATS!
SOLITAS!
THERE YOU ARE! WHO ARE YOUR FRIENDS?
I'M THE LITTLE PRINCE, AND THIS IS FOX.
WHEN I MET THEM, THEY WERE WALKING IN THE RAIN--CAN YOU BELIEVE IT?
ANIMA! IT'S TIME!
I'M SORRY, I HAVE TO GO! SEE YOU AFTER THE SHOW!
HOW UNUSUAL! YOUR THEATER IS BUILT OVER A WELL!

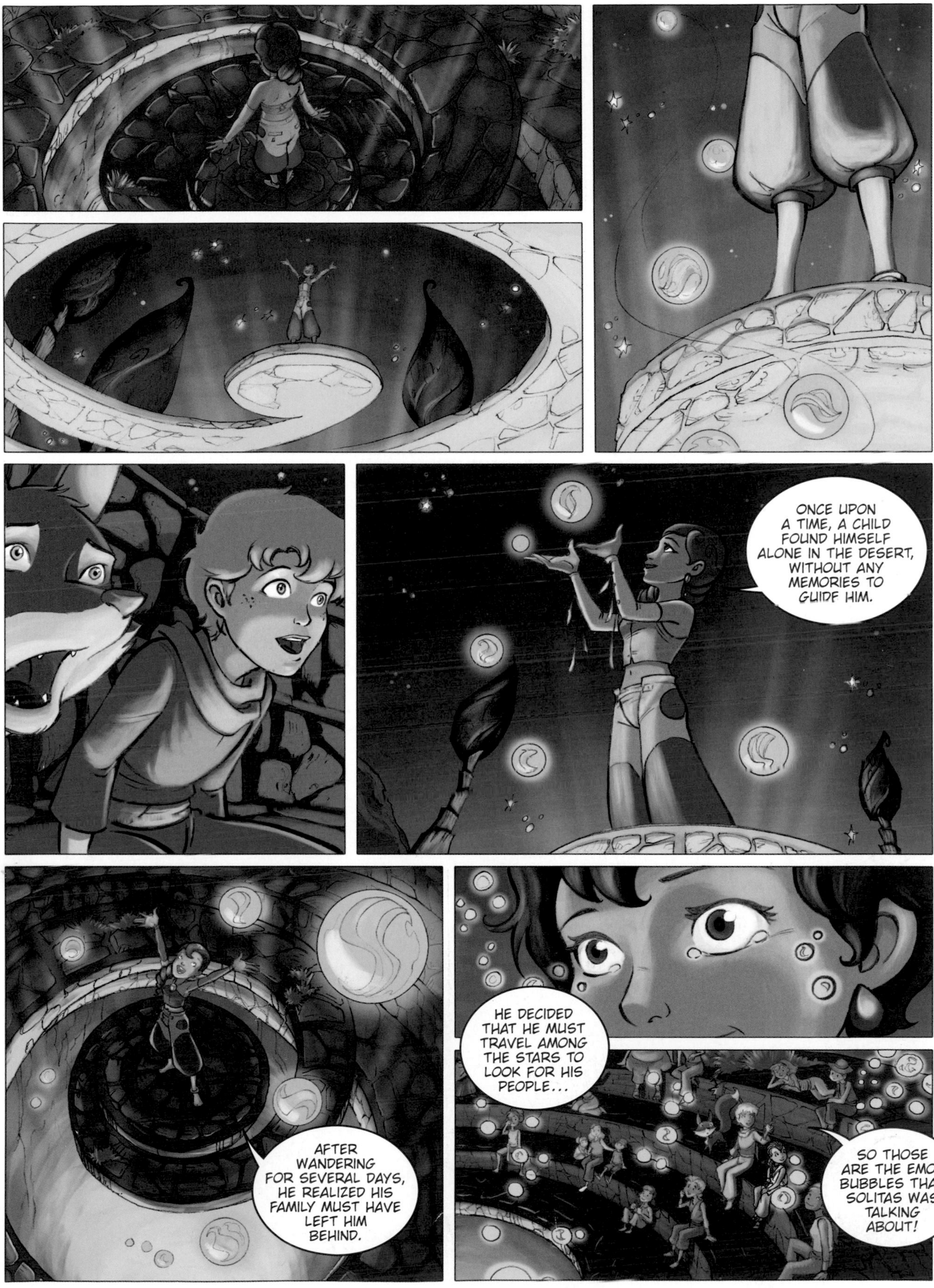
ONCE UPON A TIME, A CHILD FOUND HIMSELF ALONE IN THE DESERT, WITHOUT ANY MEMORIES TO GUIDF HIM.
AFTER WANDERING FOR SEVERAL DAYS, HE REALIZED HIS FAMILY MUST HAVE LEFT HIM BEHIND.
HE DECIDED THAT HE MUST TRAVEL AMONG THE STARS TO LOOK FOR HIS PEOPLE...
SO THOSE ARE THE EMO-BUBBLES THAT SOLITAS WAS TALKING ABOUT!

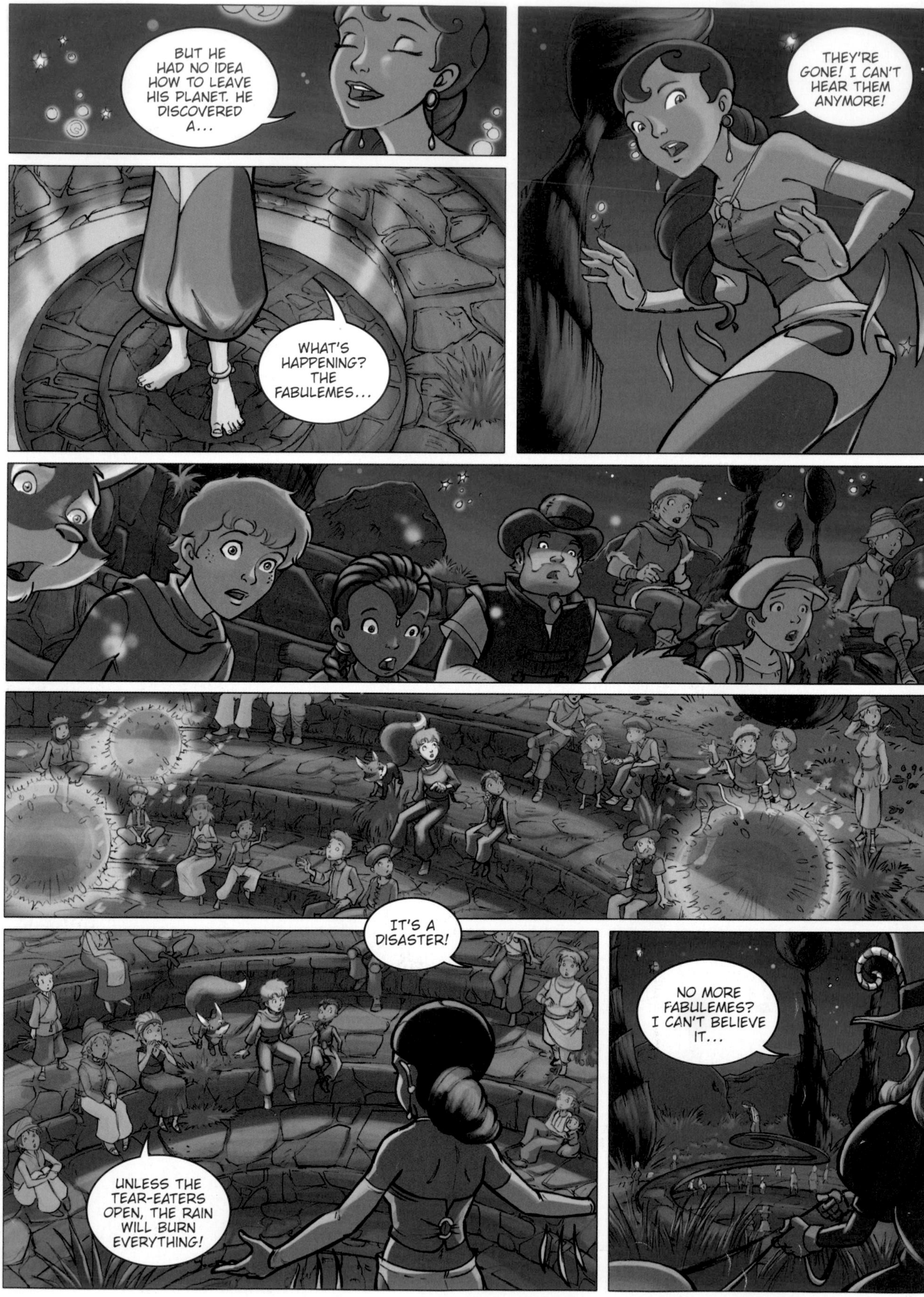
BUT HE HAD NO IDEA HOW TO LEAVE HIS PLANET. HE DISCOVERED A...
THEY'RE GONE! I CAN'T HEAR THEM ANYMORE!
WHAT'S HAPPENING? THE FABULEMES...
IT'S A DISASTER!
UNLESS THE TEAR-EATERS OPEN, THE RAIN WILL BURN EVERYTHING!
NO MORE FABULEMES? I CAN'T BELIEVE IT...

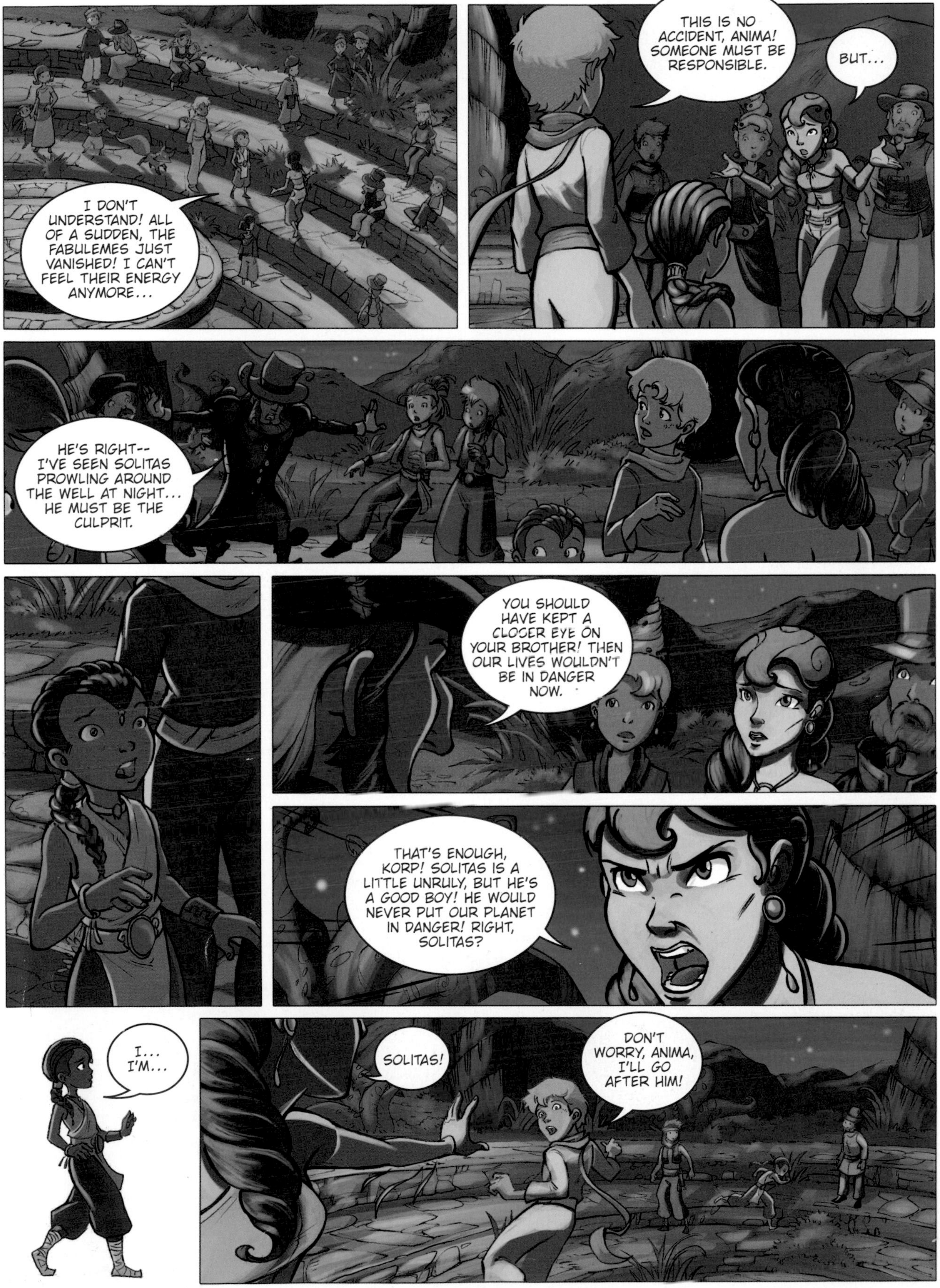
I DON'T UNDERSTAND! ALL OF A SUDDEN, THE FABULEMES JUST VANISHED! I CAN'T FEEL THEIR ENERGY ANYMORE...
THIS IS NO ACCIDENT, ANIMA! SOMEONE MUST BE RESPONSIBLE.
BUT...
HE'S RIGHT-- I'VE SEEN SOLITAS PROWLING AROUND THE WELL AT NIGHT... HE MUST BE THE CULPRIT.
YOU SHOULD HAVE KEPT A CLOSER EYE ON YOUR BROTHER! THEN OUR LIVES WOULDN'T BE IN DANGER NOW.
THAT'S ENOUGH, KORP! SOLITAS IS A LITTLE UNRULY, BUT HE'S A GOOD BOY! HE WOULD NEVER PUT OUR PLANET IN DANGER! RIGHT, SOLITAS?
I... I'M...
SOLITAS!
DON'T WORRY, ANIMA, I'LL GO AFTER HIM!

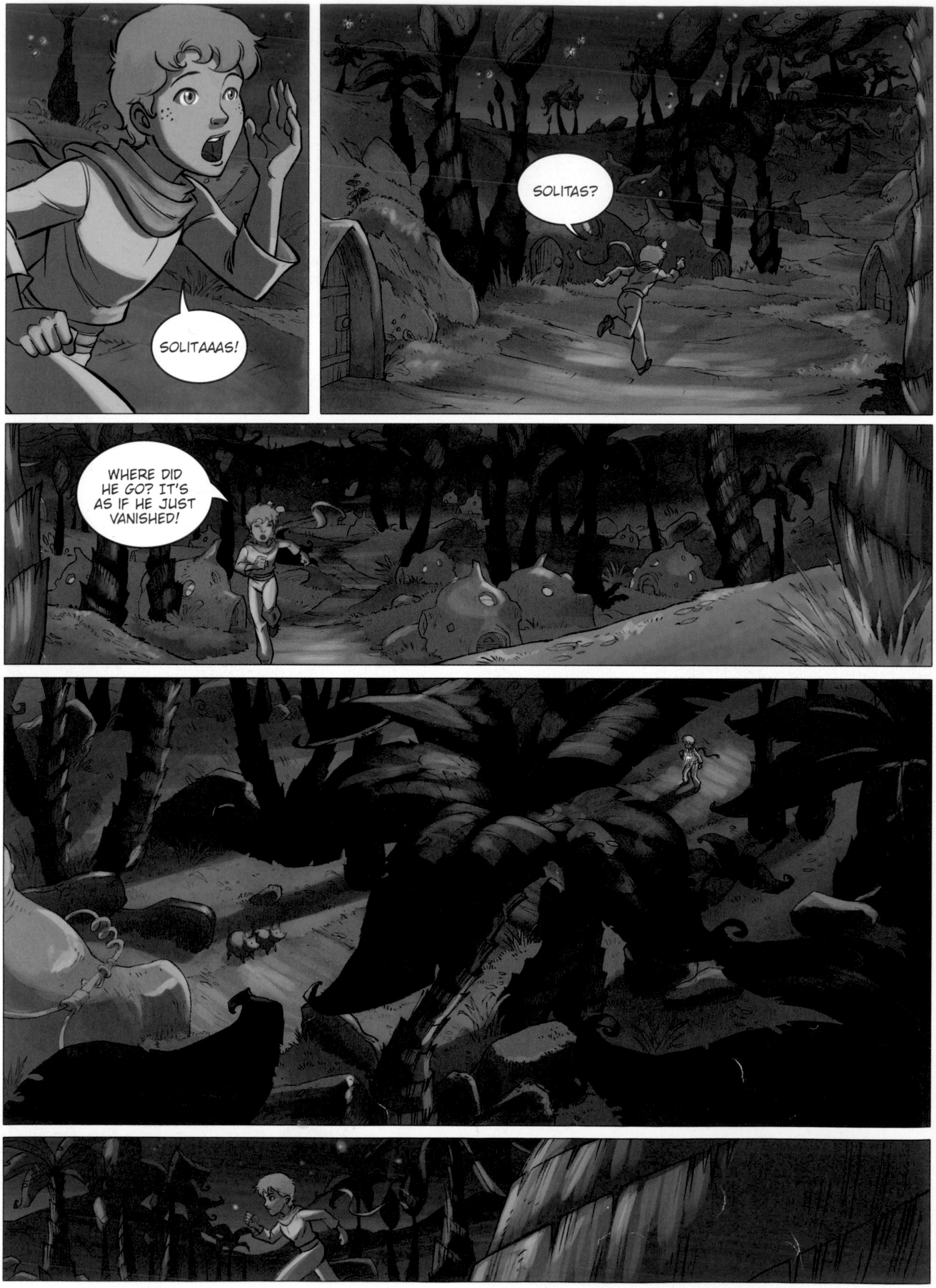
SOLITAAAS!
SOLITAS?
WHERE DID HE GO? IT'S AS IF HE JUST VANISHED!

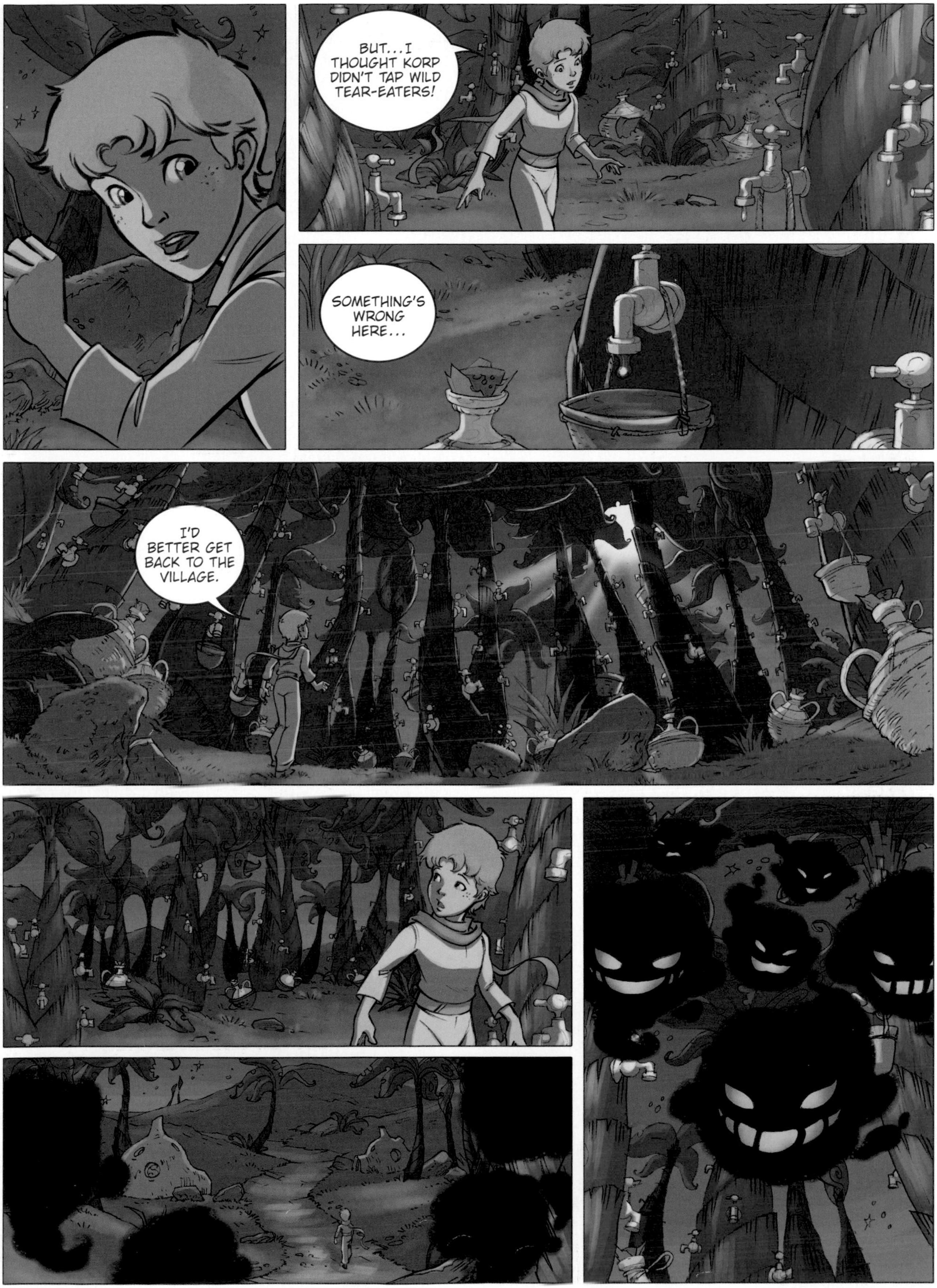
BUT... I THOUGHT KORP DIDN'T TAP WILD TEAR-EATERS!
SOMETHING'S WRONG HERE...
I'D BETTER GET BACK TO THE VILLAGE.

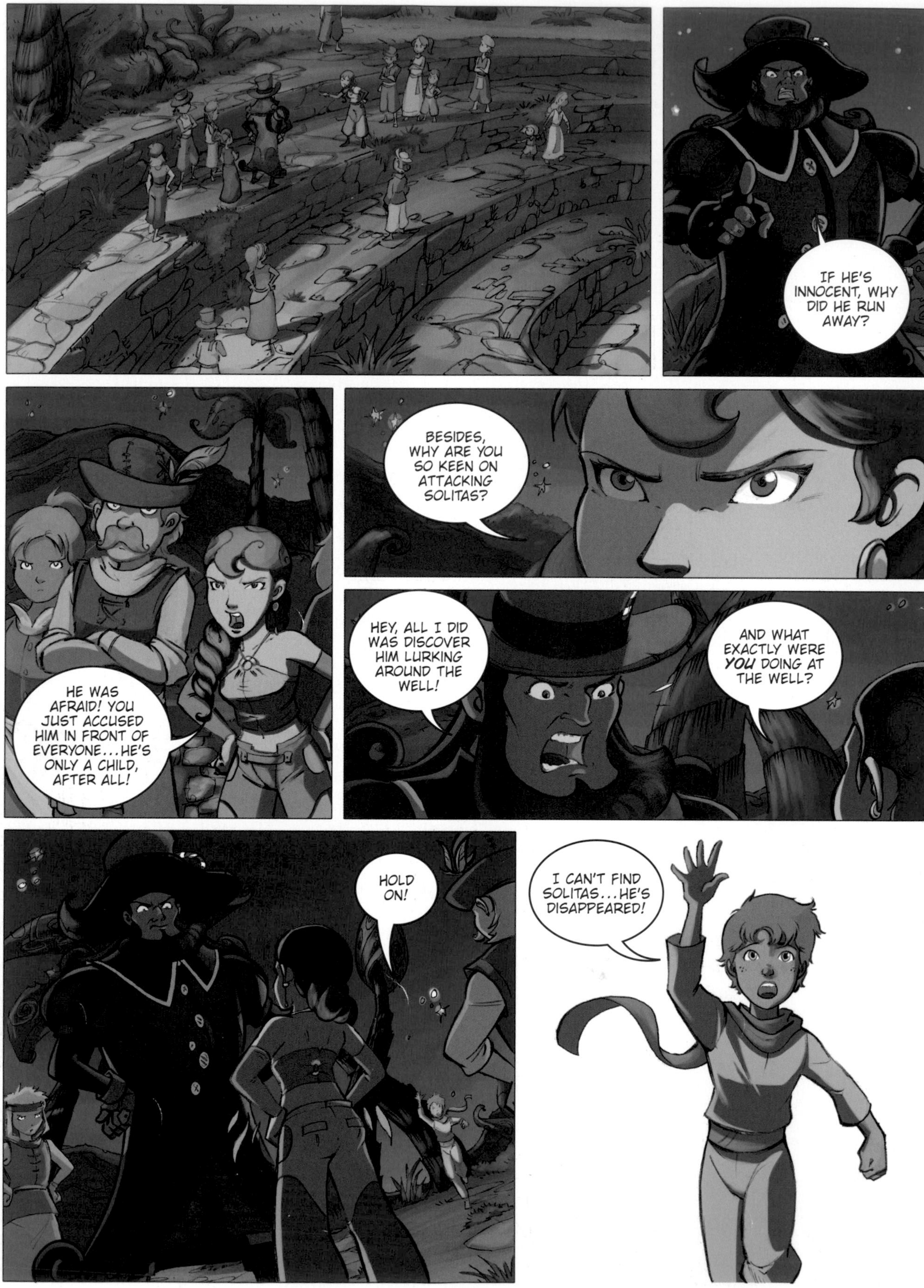
IF HE'S INNOCENT, WHY DID HE RUN AWAY?
HE WAS AFRAID! YOU JUST ACCUSED HIM IN FRONT OF EVERYONE... HE'S ONLY A CHILD, AFTER ALL!
BESIDES, WHY ARE YOU SO KEEN ON ATTACKING SOLITAS?
HEY, ALL I DID WAS DISCOVER HIM LURKING AROUND THE WELL!
AND WHAT EXACTLY WERE *YOU* DOING AT THE WELL?
HOLD ON!
I CAN'T FIND SOLITAS... HE'S DISAPPEARED!

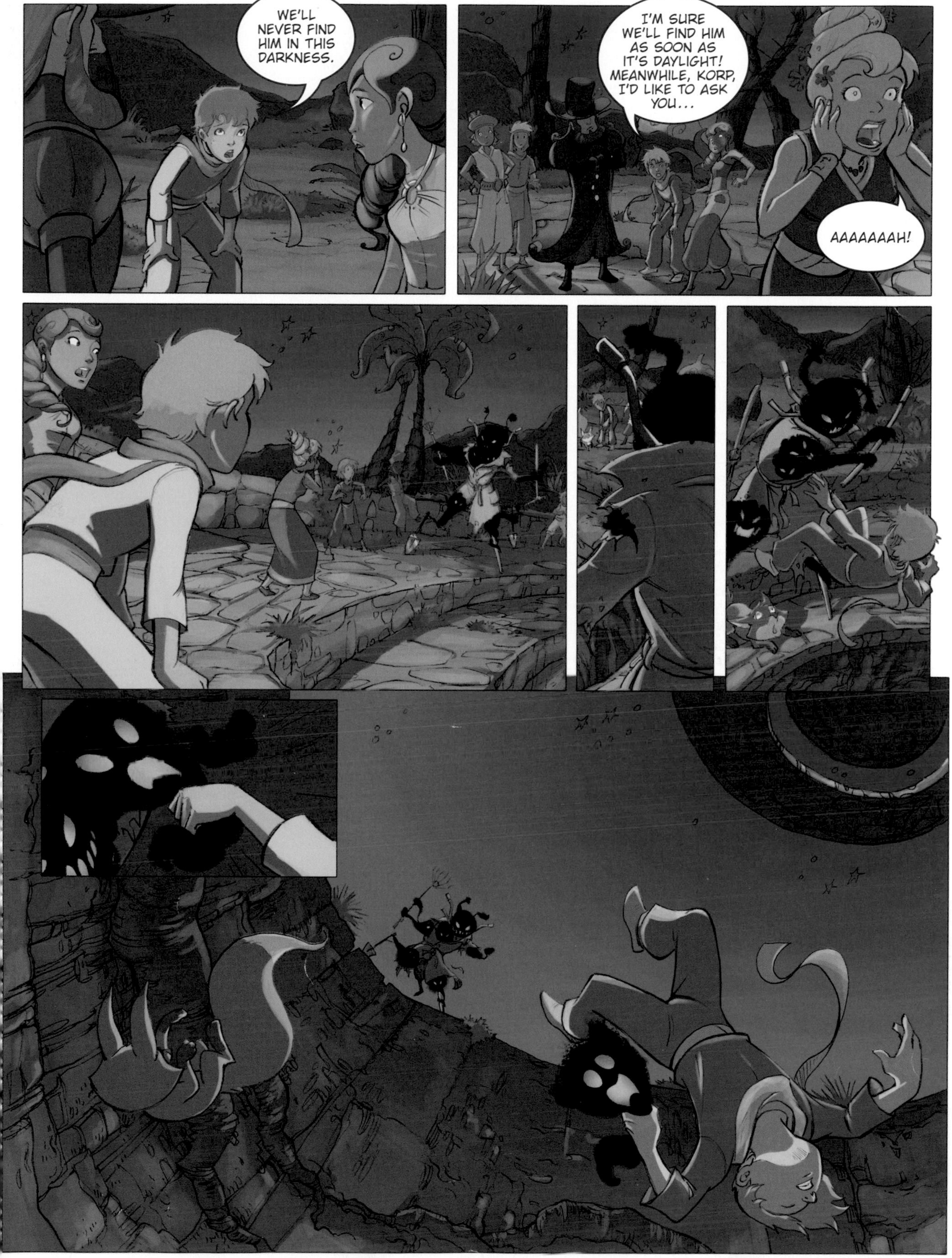
WE'LL NEVER FIND HIM IN THIS DARKNESS.
I'M SURE WE'LL FIND HIM AS SOON AS IT'S DAYLIGHT! MEANWHILE, KORP, I'D LIKE TO ASK YOU...
AAAAAAAH!

AAAAAAH!

LITTLE PRINCE!

OW!

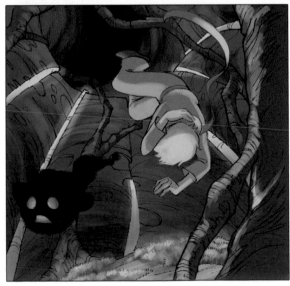

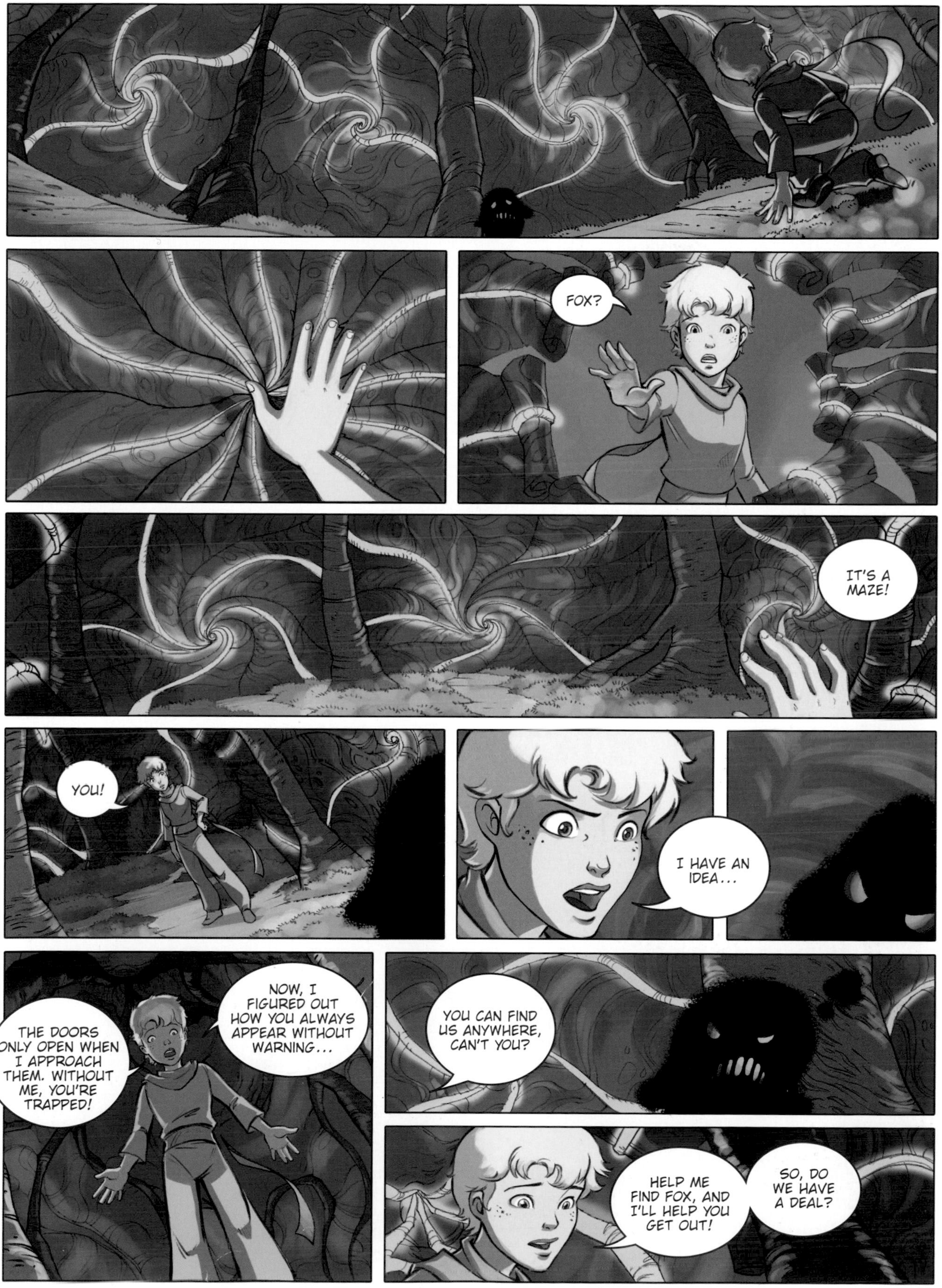
FOX?
IT'S A MAZE!
YOU!
I HAVE AN IDEA...
THE DOORS ONLY OPEN WHEN I APPROACH THEM. WITHOUT ME, YOU'RE TRAPPED!
NOW, I FIGURED OUT HOW YOU ALWAYS APPEAR WITHOUT WARNING...
YOU CAN FIND US ANYWHERE, CAN'T YOU?
HELP ME FIND FOX, AND I'LL HELP YOU GET OUT!
SO, DO WE HAVE A DEAL?

GOOD!

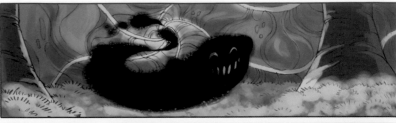

LET'S GO!

IS HE HERE?

FOX?

WHERE ARE YOU?

LITTLE PRINCE?

FOX! THERE YOU ARE!

WATCH OUT, LITTLE PRINCE! THERE'S A GLOOMIE SNEAKING UP BEHIND YOU!

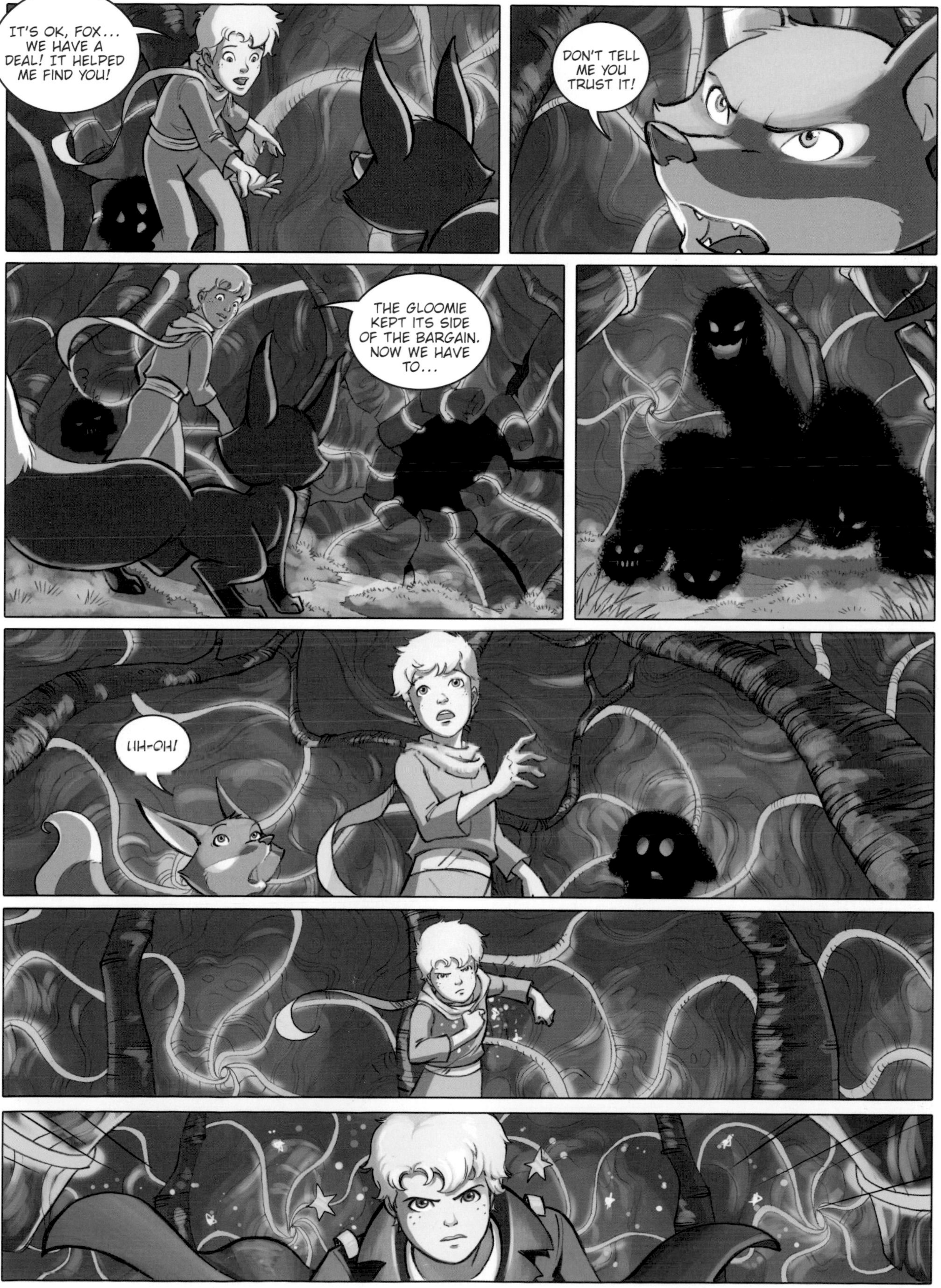
IT'S OK, FOX... WE HAVE A DEAL! IT HELPED ME FIND YOU!
DON'T TELL ME YOU TRUST IT!
THE GLOOMIE KEPT ITS SIDE OF THE BARGAIN. NOW WE HAVE TO...
UH-OH!

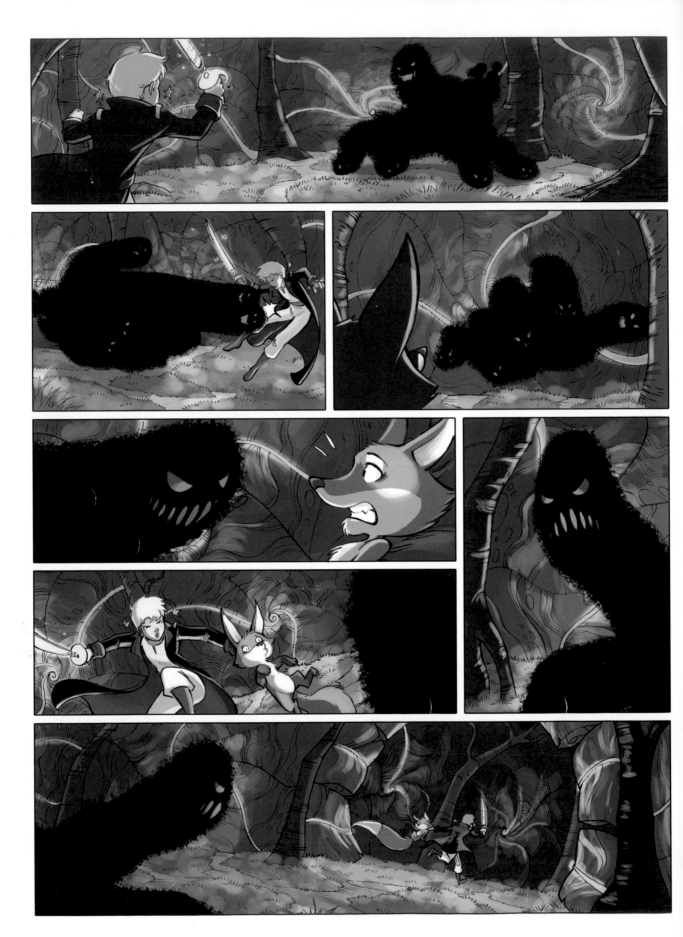

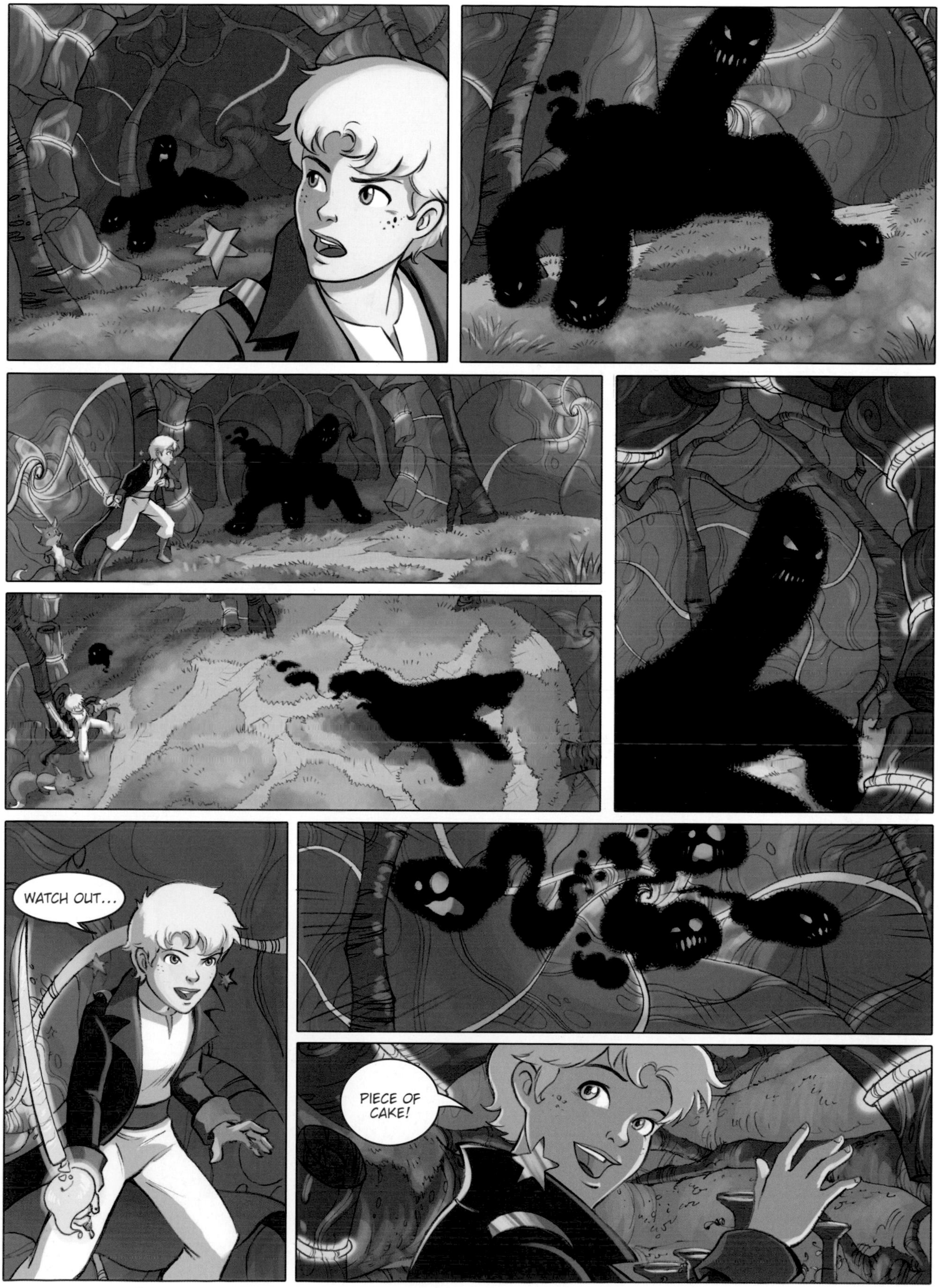
WATCH OUT...
PIECE OF CAKE!

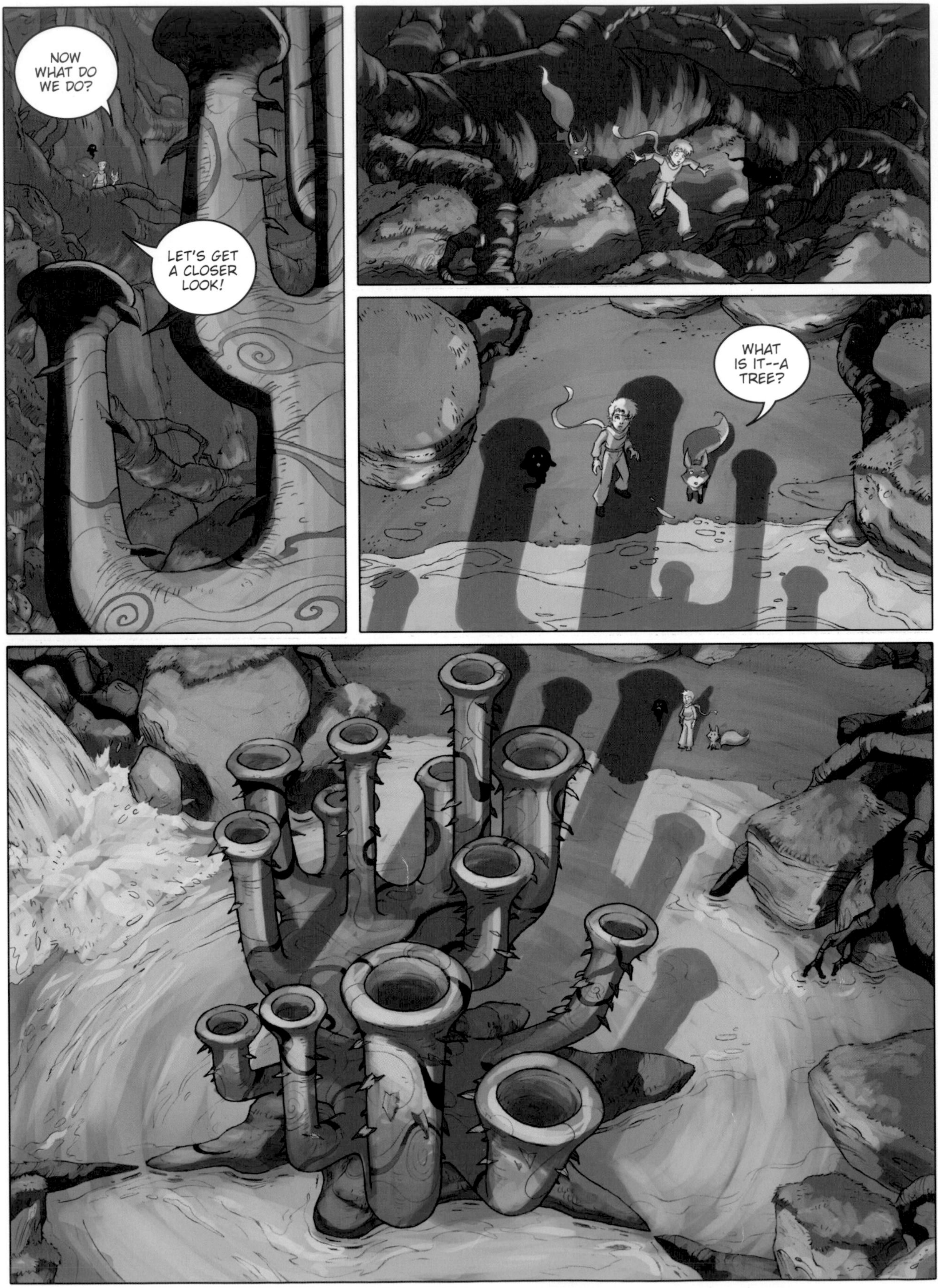
NOW WHAT DO WE DO?
LET'S GET A CLOSER LOOK!
WHAT IS IT--A TREE?

THIS MUST BE WHERE THE FABULEMES COME FROM...

WHAT?

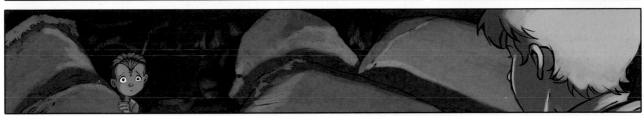

SOLITAS! SO HERE YOU ARE! WHY DID YOU RUN AWAY?

I... I CAN EXPLAIN!

I'M SO SORRY! I'VE DONE A TERRIBLE THING!

YOU CAN TRUST US, SOLITAS... WE'RE HERE TO HELP.

A WHILE AGO, BY ACCIDENT, I FOUND A SECRET PASSAGE NEAR KORP'S HOUSE...

...YOU KEPT COMING BACK HERE, DIDN'T YOU?

...AND IT LED ME HERE. I KNOW IT'S AGAINST THE LAW TO ENTER THE WELL, BUT...

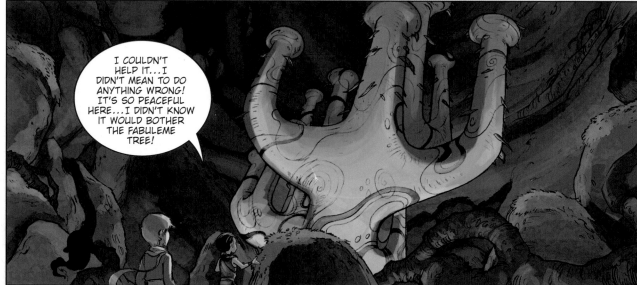

I COULDN'T HELP IT...I DIDN'T MEAN TO DO ANYTHING WRONG! IT'S SO PEACEFUL HERE...I DIDN'T KNOW IT WOULD BOTHER THE FABULEME TREE!

A FEW DAYS AGO, THE WATER BEGAN TO RISE! I DON'T KNOW WHY, BUT I'M AFRAID IT WAS MY FAULT!

I DON'T THINK YOU'RE TO BLAME... HAVE YOU EVER HEARD OF THE SNAKE?

THE WHAT?

30

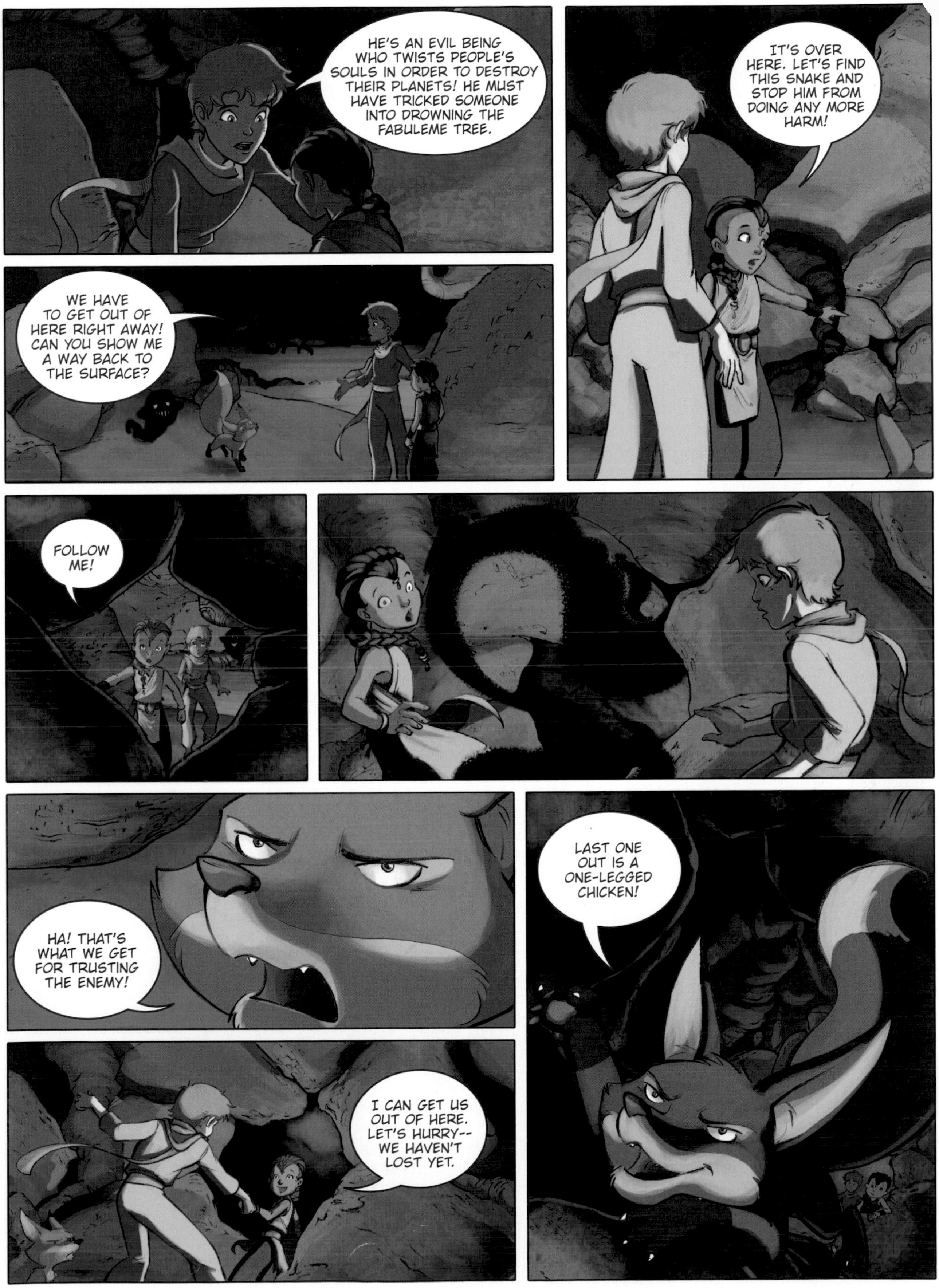
HE'S AN EVIL BEING WHO TWISTS PEOPLE'S SOULS IN ORDER TO DESTROY THEIR PLANETS! HE MUST HAVE TRICKED SOMEONE INTO DROWNING THE FABULEME TREE.
IT'S OVER HERE. LET'S FIND THIS SNAKE AND STOP HIM FROM DOING ANY MORE HARM!
WE HAVE TO GET OUT OF HERE RIGHT AWAY! CAN YOU SHOW ME A WAY BACK TO THE SURFACE?
FOLLOW ME!
HA! THAT'S WHAT WE GET FOR TRUSTING THE ENEMY!
LAST ONE OUT IS A ONE-LEGGED CHICKEN!
I CAN GET US OUT OF HERE. LET'S HURRY-- WE HAVEN'T LOST YET.

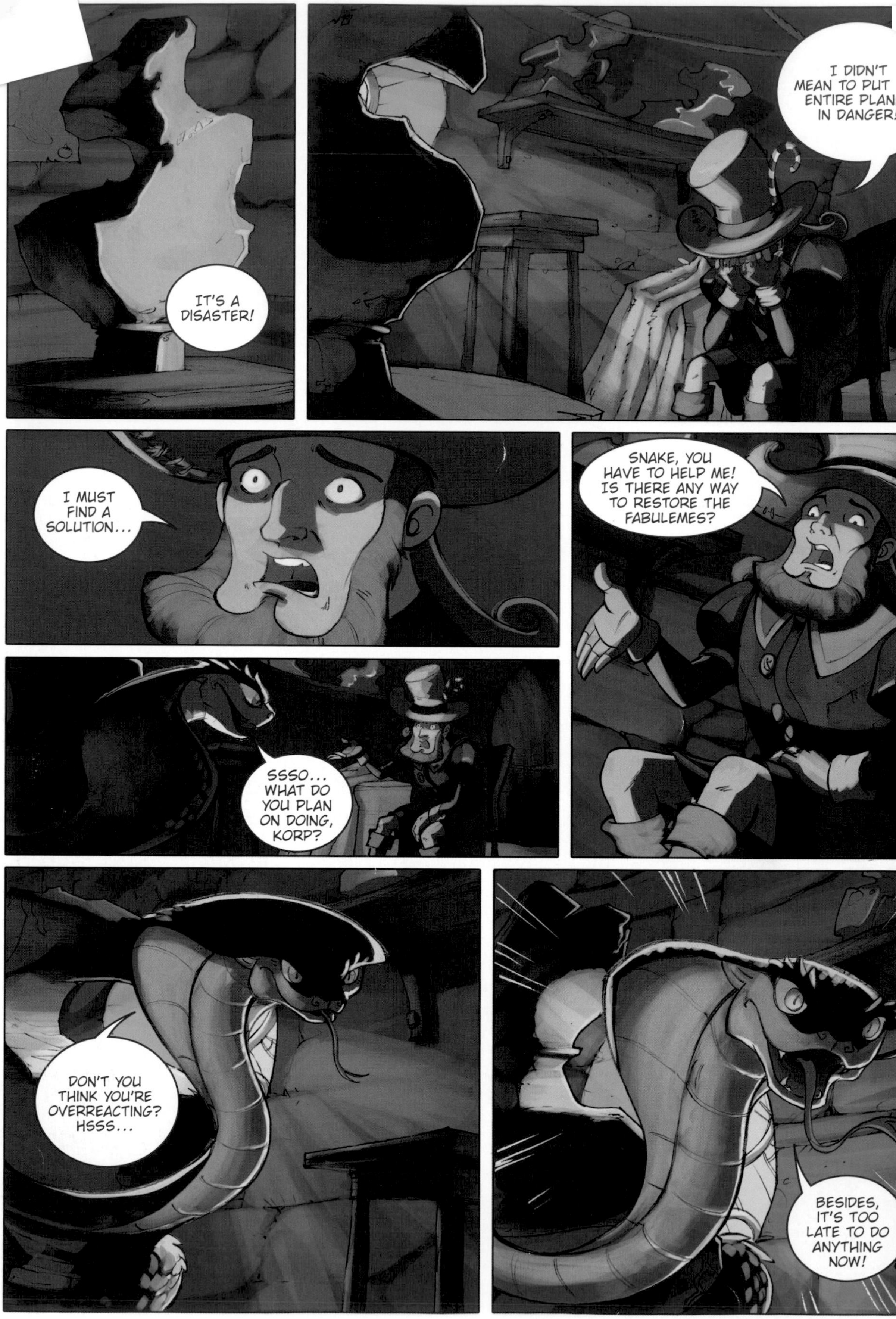
IT'S A DISASTER!
I DIDN'T MEAN TO PUT THE ENTIRE PLANET IN DANGER!
I MUST FIND A SOLUTION...
SNAKE, YOU HAVE TO HELP ME! IS THERE ANY WAY TO RESTORE THE FABULEMES?
SSSO... WHAT DO YOU PLAN ON DOING, KORP?
DON'T YOU THINK YOU'RE OVERREACTING? HSSS...
BESIDES, IT'S TOO LATE TO DO ANYTHING NOW!

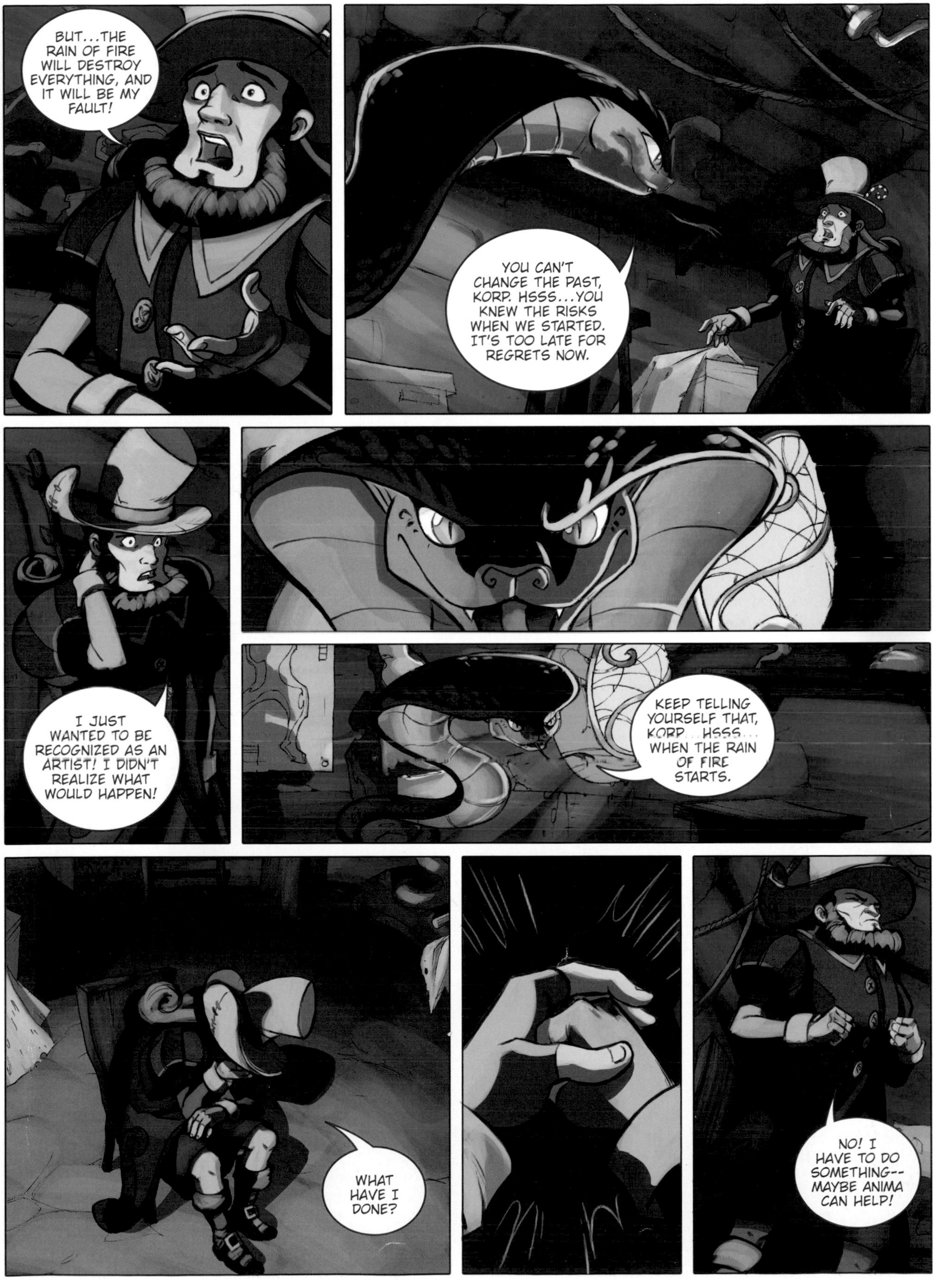
BUT...THE RAIN OF FIRE WILL DESTROY EVERYTHING, AND IT WILL BE MY FAULT!
YOU CAN'T CHANGE THE PAST, KORP. HSSS...YOU KNEW THE RISKS WHEN WE STARTED. IT'S TOO LATE FOR REGRETS NOW.
I JUST WANTED TO BE RECOGNIZED AS AN ARTIST! I DIDN'T REALIZE WHAT WOULD HAPPEN!
KEEP TELLING YOURSELF THAT, KORP...HSSS... WHEN THE RAIN OF FIRE STARTS.
WHAT HAVE I DONE?
NO! I HAVE TO DO SOMETHING-- MAYBE ANIMA CAN HELP!

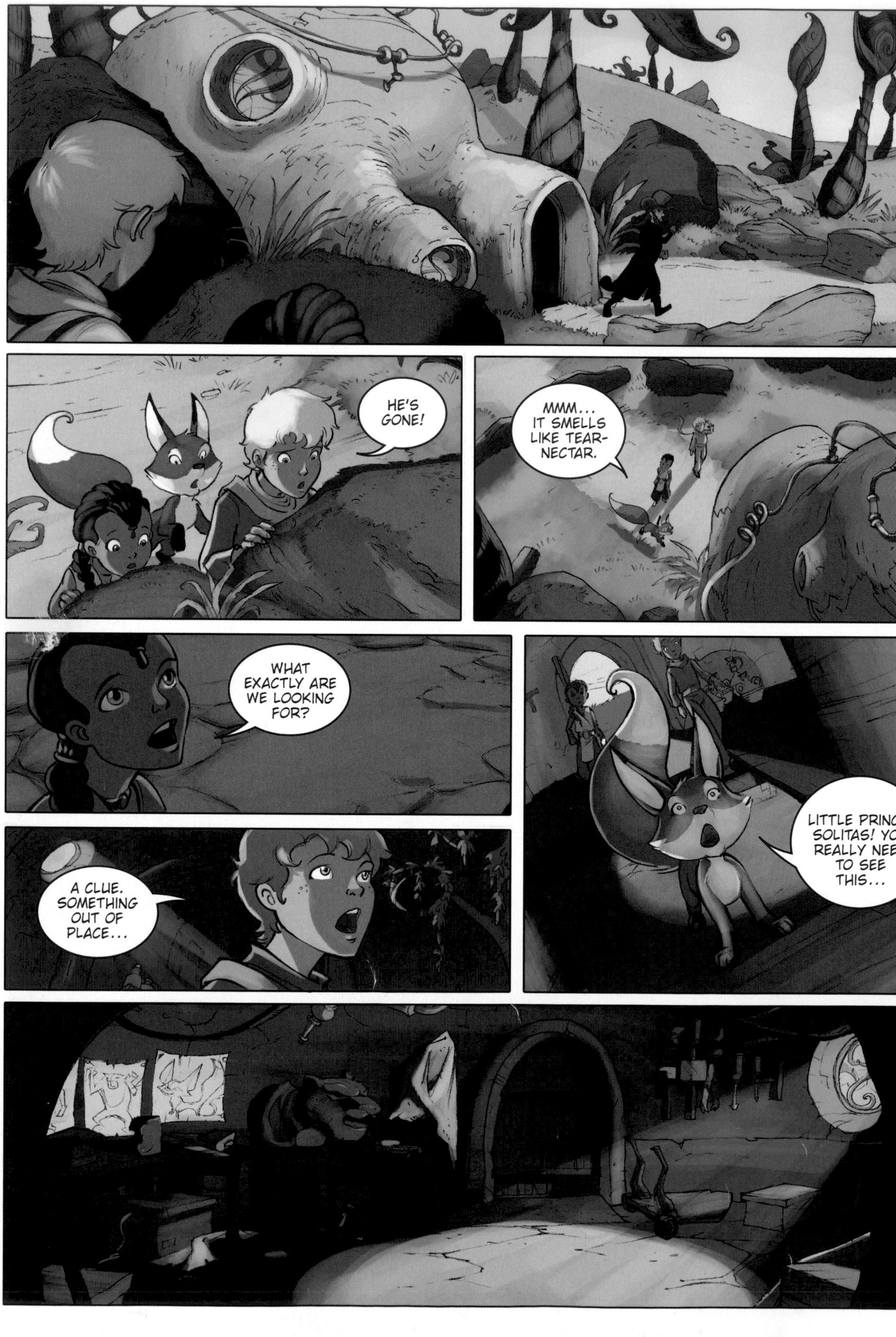
HE'S GONE!
MMM... IT SMELLS LIKE TEAR-NECTAR.
WHAT EXACTLY ARE WE LOOKING FOR?
A CLUE. SOMETHING OUT OF PLACE...
LITTLE PRINCE! SOLITAS! YOU REALLY NEED TO SEE THIS...

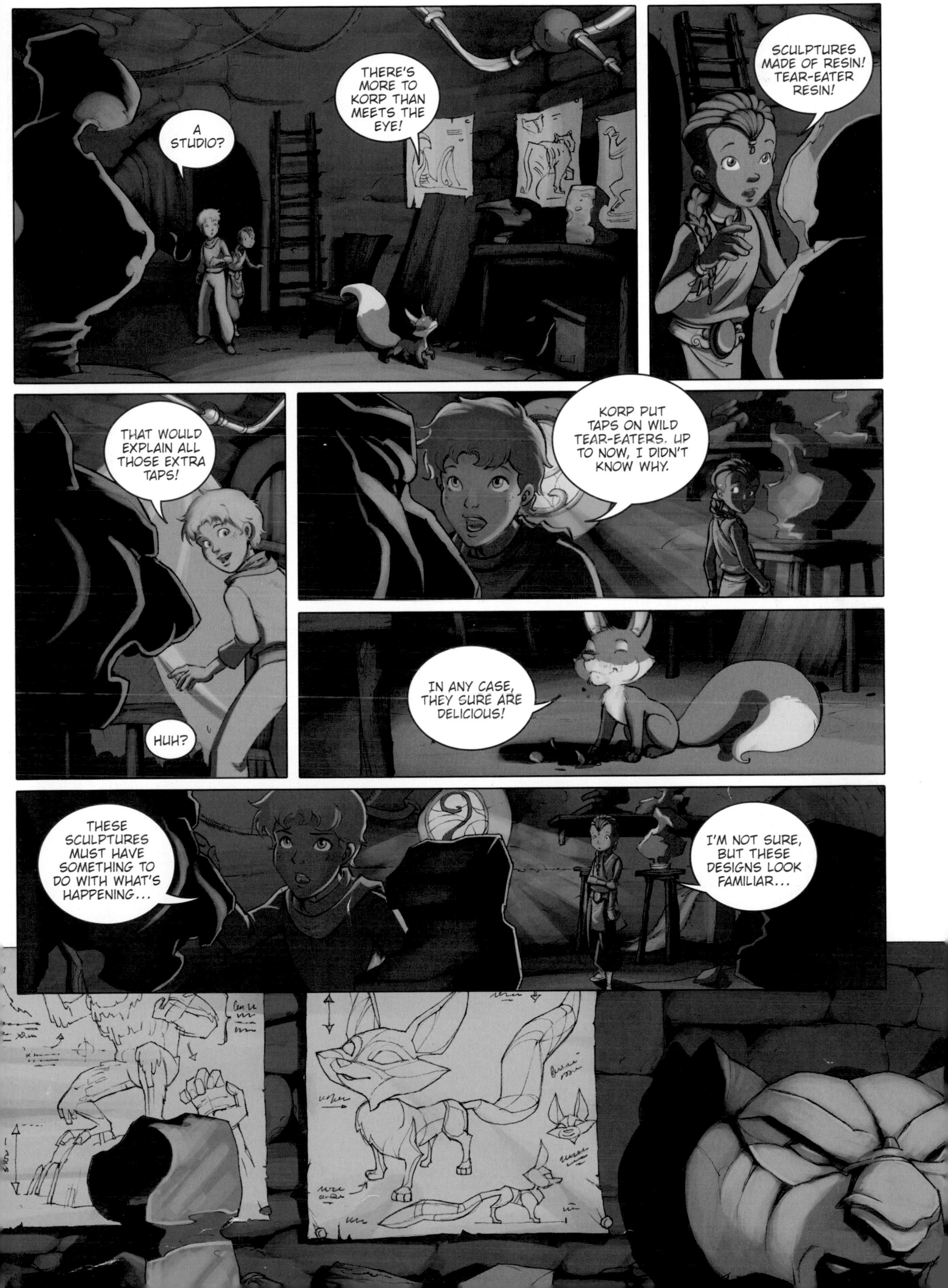
A STUDIO?
THERE'S MORE TO KORP THAN MEETS THE EYE!
SCULPTURES MADE OF RESIN! TEAR-EATER RESIN!
THAT WOULD EXPLAIN ALL THOSE EXTRA TAPS!
KORP PUT TAPS ON WILD TEAR-EATERS. UP TO NOW, I DIDN'T KNOW WHY.
IN ANY CASE, THEY SURE ARE DELICIOUS!
HUH?
THESE SCULPTURES MUST HAVE SOMETHING TO DO WITH WHAT'S HAPPENING...
I'M NOT SURE, BUT THESE DESIGNS LOOK FAMILIAR...

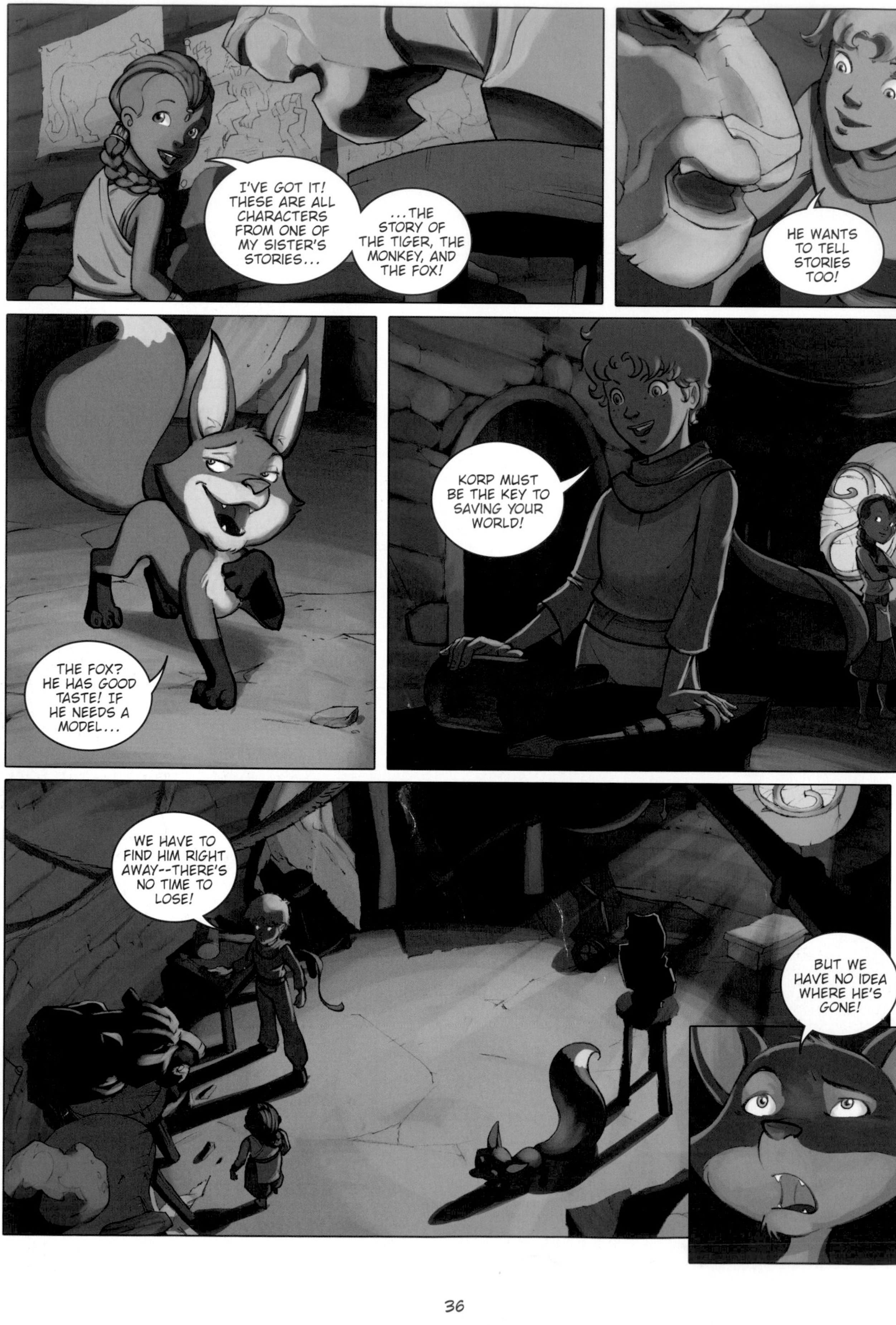
I'VE GOT IT! THESE ARE ALL CHARACTERS FROM ONE OF MY SISTER'S STORIES...
...THE STORY OF THE TIGER, THE MONKEY, AND THE FOX!
HE WANTS TO TELL STORIES TOO!
THE FOX? HE HAS GOOD TASTE! IF HE NEEDS A MODEL...
KORP MUST BE THE KEY TO SAVING YOUR WORLD!
WE HAVE TO FIND HIM RIGHT AWAY--THERE'S NO TIME TO LOSE!
BUT WE HAVE NO IDEA WHERE HE'S GONE!

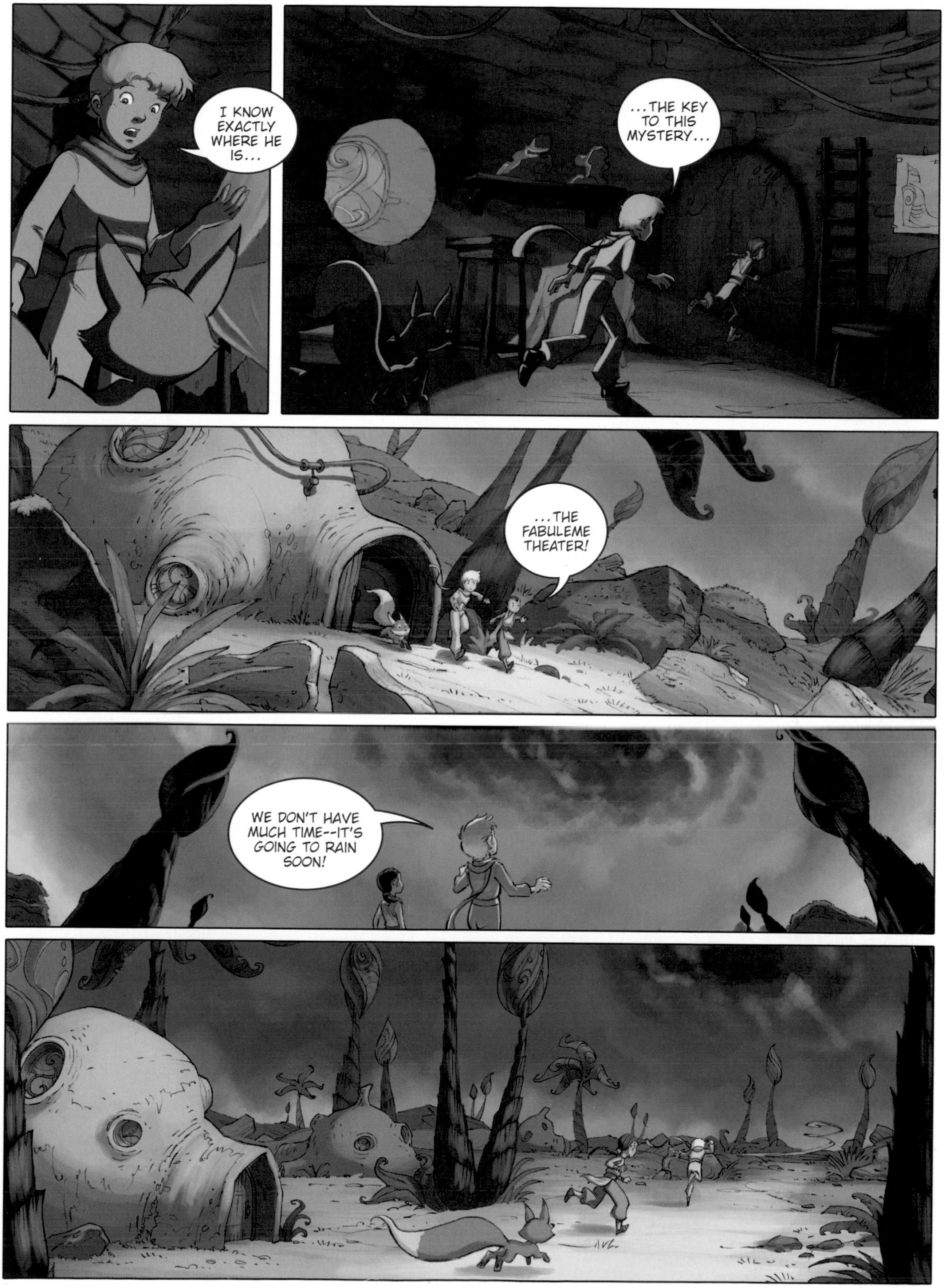
I KNOW EXACTLY WHERE HE IS...
...THE KEY TO THIS MYSTERY...
...THE FABULEME THEATER!
WE DON'T HAVE MUCH TIME--IT'S GOING TO RAIN SOON!

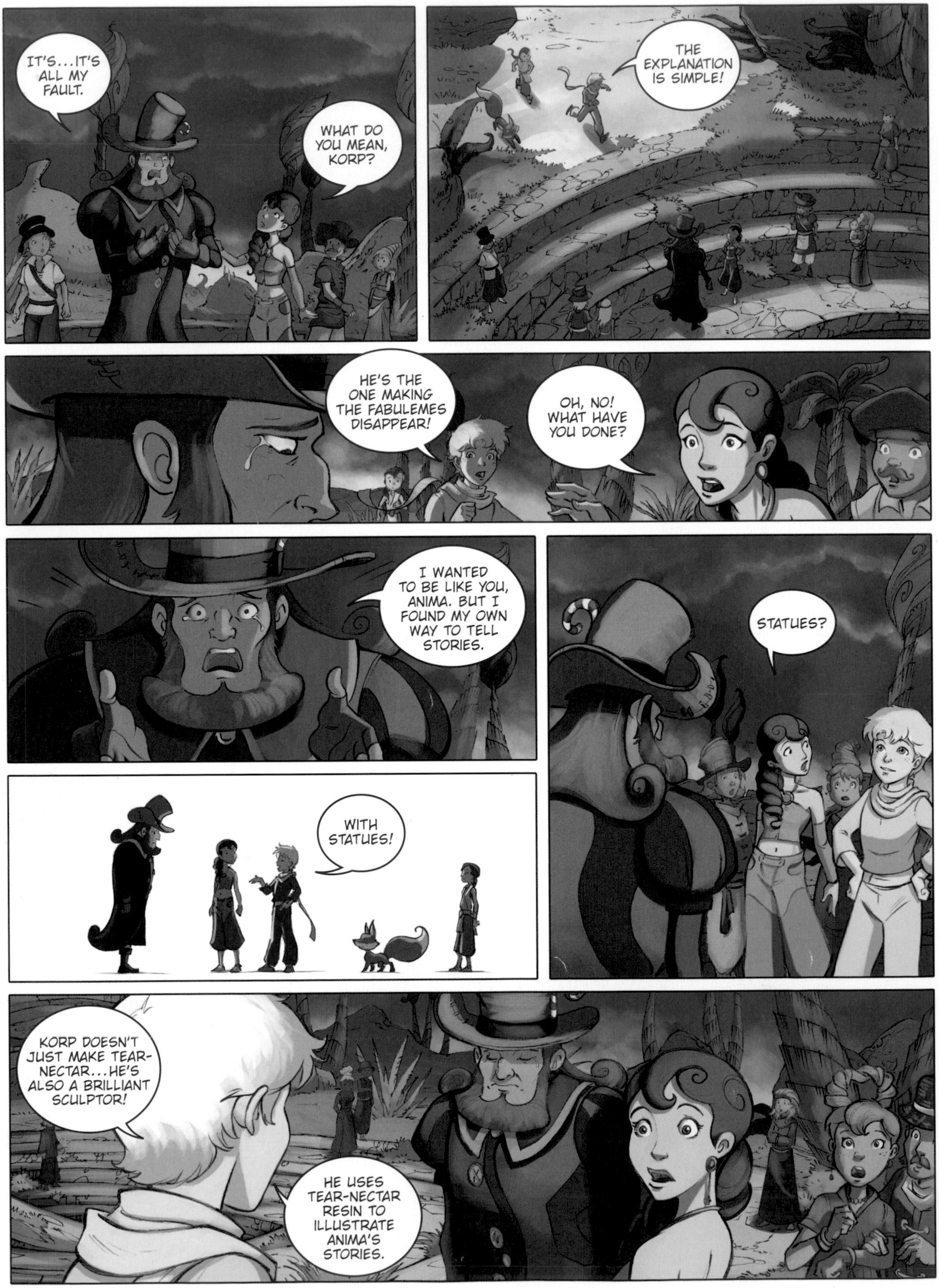
IT'S...IT'S ALL MY FAULT.
WHAT DO YOU MEAN, KORP?
THE EXPLANATION IS SIMPLE!
HE'S THE ONE MAKING THE FABULEMES DISAPPEAR!
OH, NO! WHAT HAVE YOU DONE?
I WANTED TO BE LIKE YOU, ANIMA. BUT I FOUND MY OWN WAY TO TELL STORIES.
WITH STATUES!
STATUES?
KORP DOESN'T JUST MAKE TEAR-NECTAR...HE'S ALSO A BRILLIANT SCULPTOR!
HE USES TEAR-NECTAR RESIN TO ILLUSTRATE ANIMA'S STORIES.

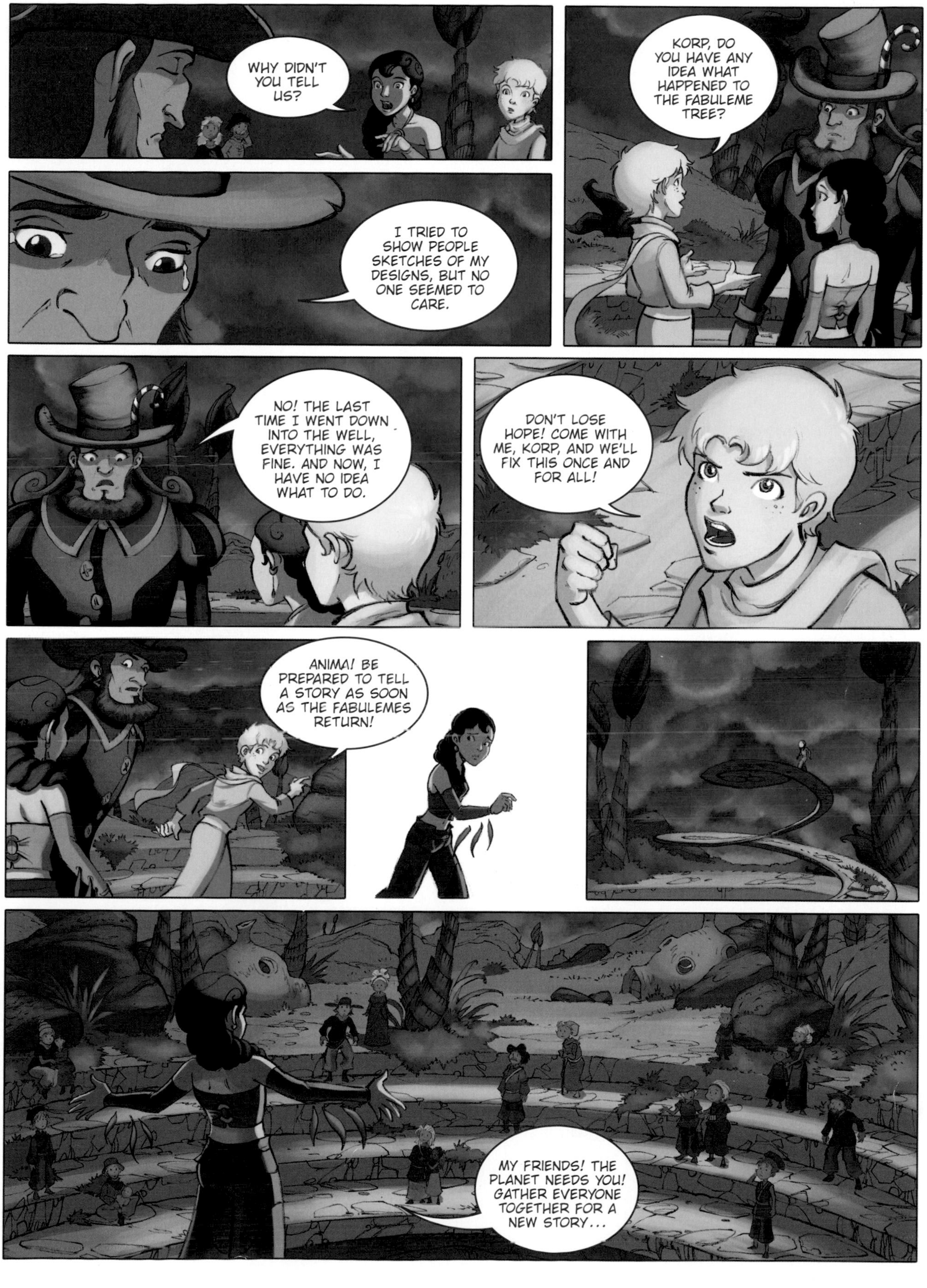
WHY DIDN'T YOU TELL US?
KORP, DO YOU HAVE ANY IDEA WHAT HAPPENED TO THE FABULEME TREE?
I TRIED TO SHOW PEOPLE SKETCHES OF MY DESIGNS, BUT NO ONE SEEMED TO CARE.
NO! THE LAST TIME I WENT DOWN INTO THE WELL, EVERYTHING WAS FINE. AND NOW, I HAVE NO IDEA WHAT TO DO.
DON'T LOSE HOPE! COME WITH ME, KORP, AND WE'LL FIX THIS ONCE AND FOR ALL!
ANIMA! BE PREPARED TO TELL A STORY AS SOON AS THE FABULEMES RETURN!
MY FRIENDS! THE PLANET NEEDS YOU! GATHER EVERYONE TOGETHER FOR A NEW STORY...

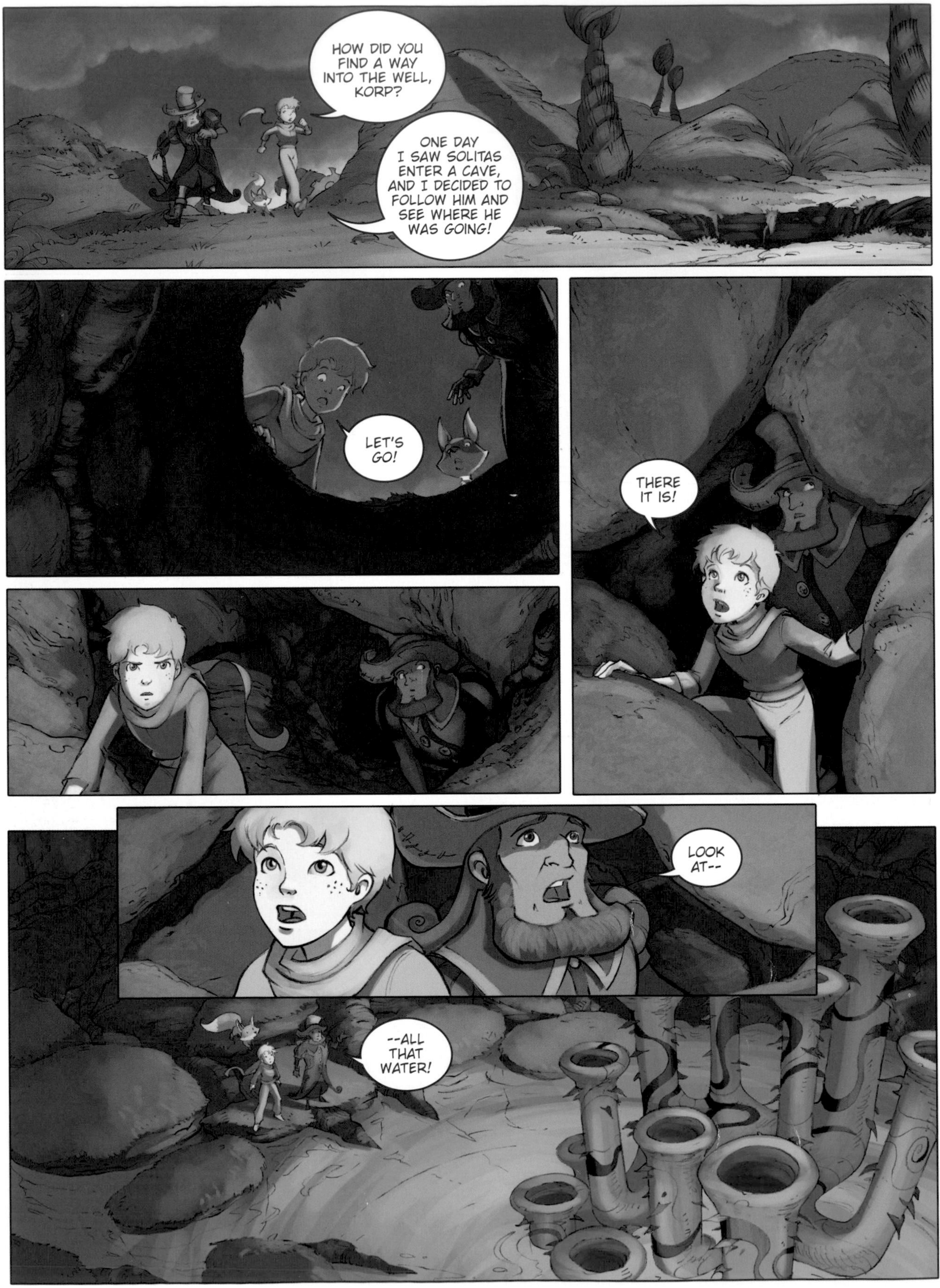
HOW DID YOU FIND A WAY INTO THE WELL, KORP?
ONE DAY I SAW SOLITAS ENTER A CAVE, AND I DECIDED TO FOLLOW HIM AND SEE WHERE HE WAS GOING!
LET'S GO!
THERE IT IS!
LOOK AT--
--ALL THAT WATER!

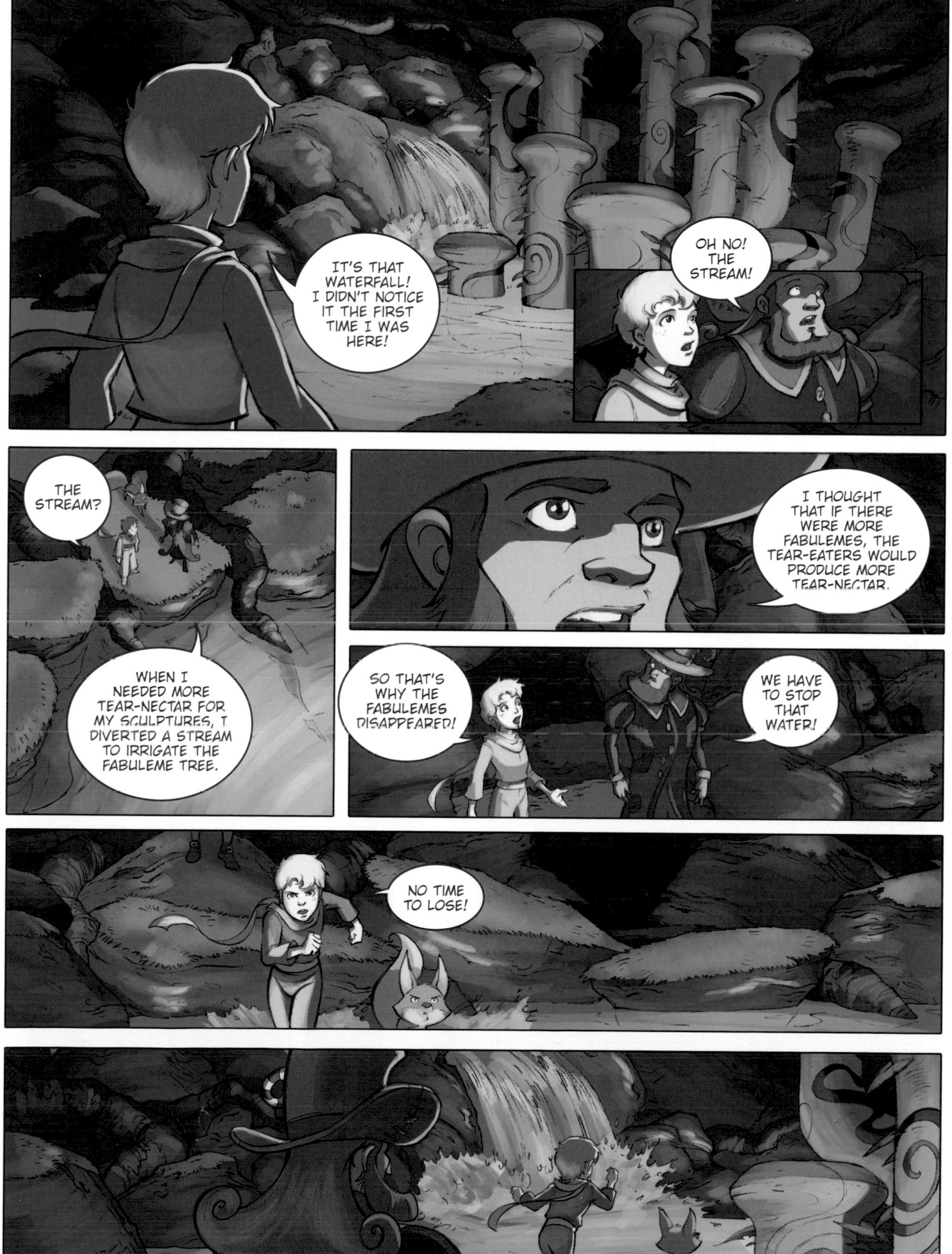
IT'S THAT WATERFALL! I DIDN'T NOTICE IT THE FIRST TIME I WAS HERE!
OH NO! THE STREAM!
THE STREAM?
WHEN I NEEDED MORE TEAR-NECTAR FOR MY SCULPTURES, I DIVERTED A STREAM TO IRRIGATE THE FABULEME TREE.
I THOUGHT THAT IF THERE WERE MORE FABULEMES, THE TEAR-EATERS WOULD PRODUCE MORE TEAR-NECTAR.
SO THAT'S WHY THE FABULEMES DISAPPEARED!
WE HAVE TO STOP THAT WATER!
NO TIME TO LOSE!

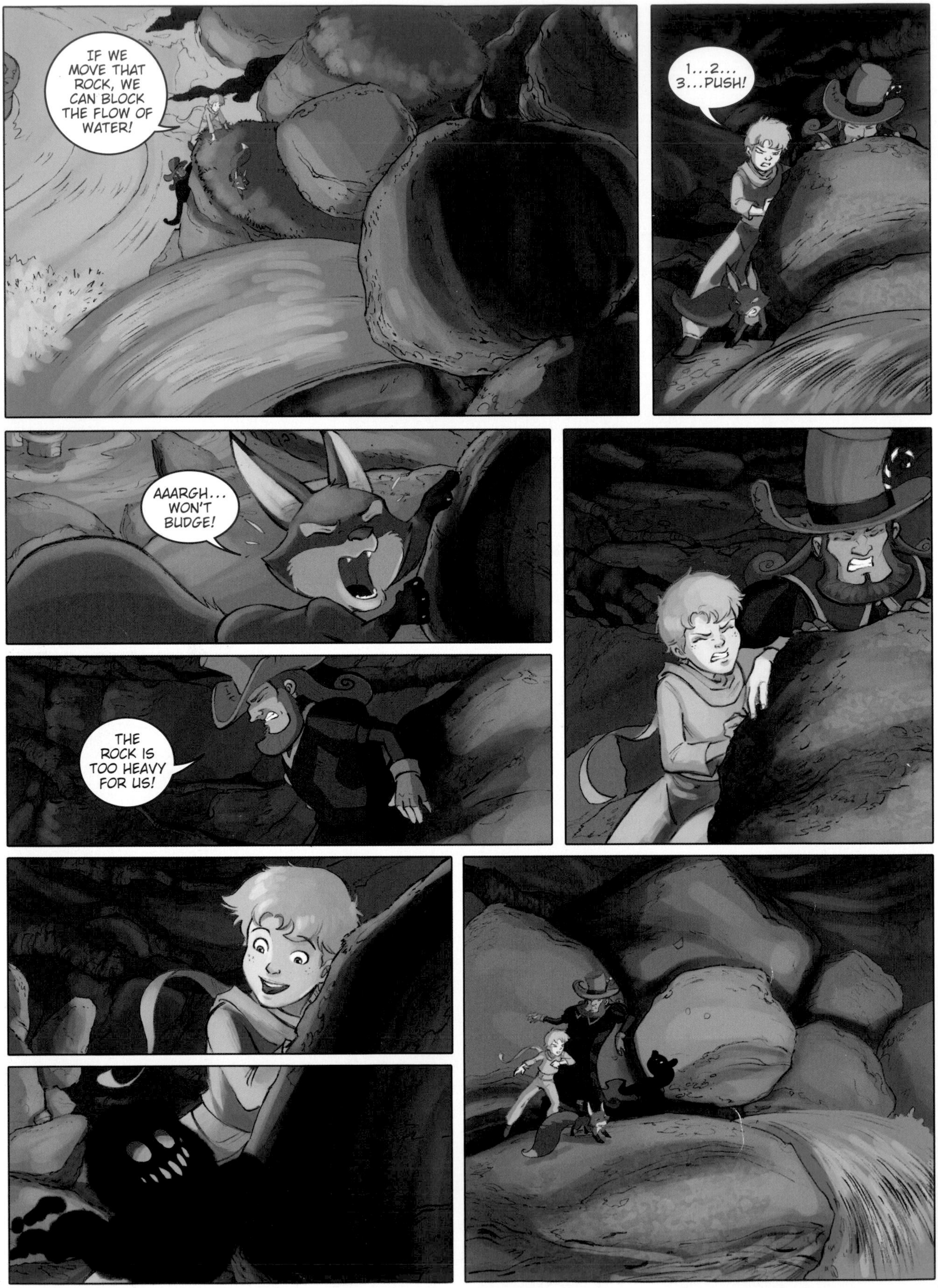
IF WE MOVE THAT ROCK, WE CAN BLOCK THE FLOW OF WATER!
1...2... 3...PUSH!
AAARGH... WON'T BUDGE!
THE ROCK IS TOO HEAVY FOR US!

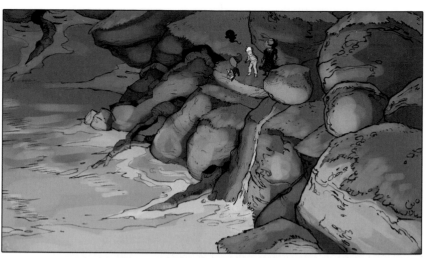

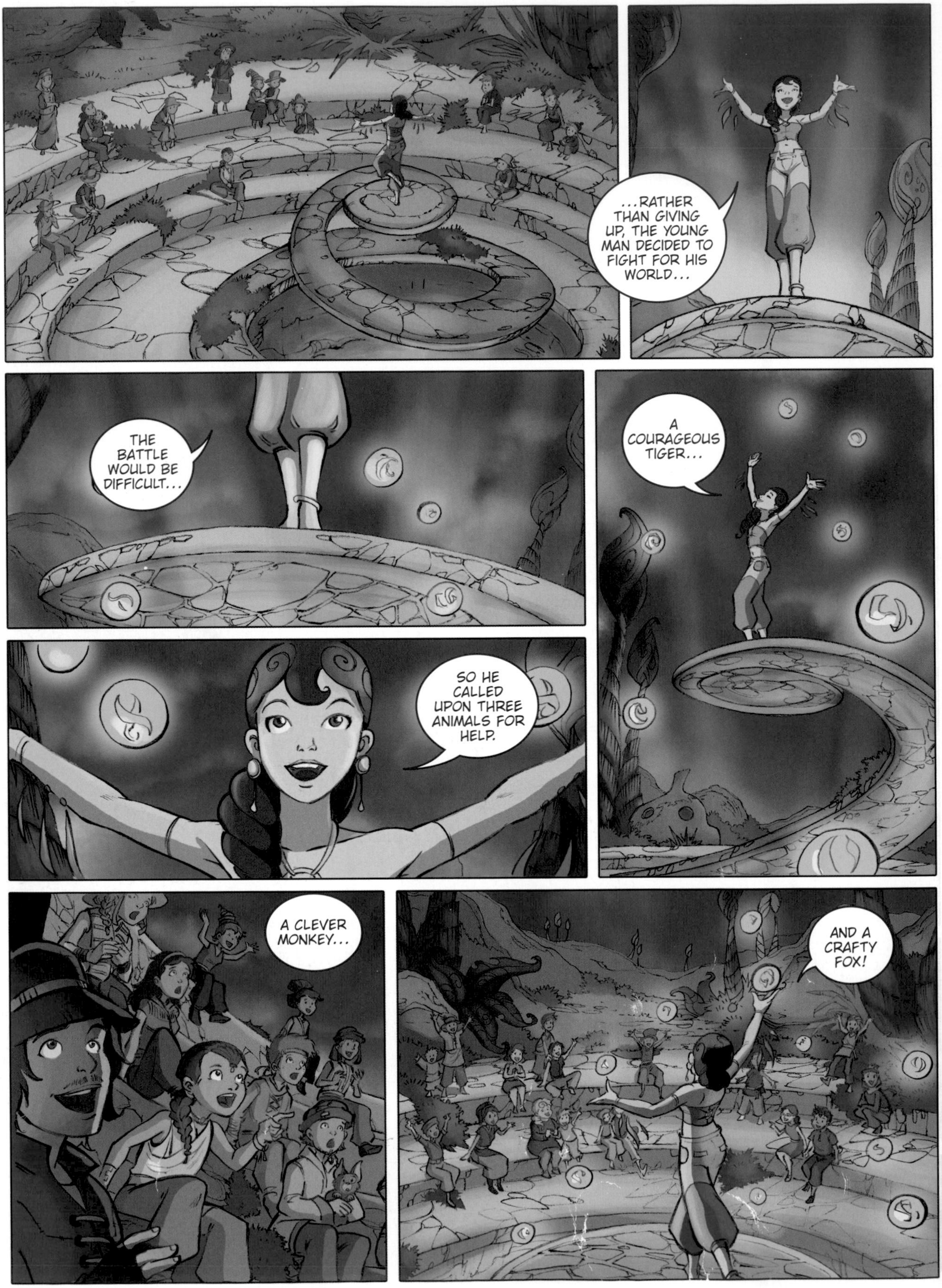
...RATHER THAN GIVING UP, THE YOUNG MAN DECIDED TO FIGHT FOR HIS WORLD...
THE BATTLE WOULD BE DIFFICULT...
A COURAGEOUS TIGER...
SO HE CALLED UPON THREE ANIMALS FOR HELP.
A CLEVER MONKEY...
AND A CRAFTY FOX!

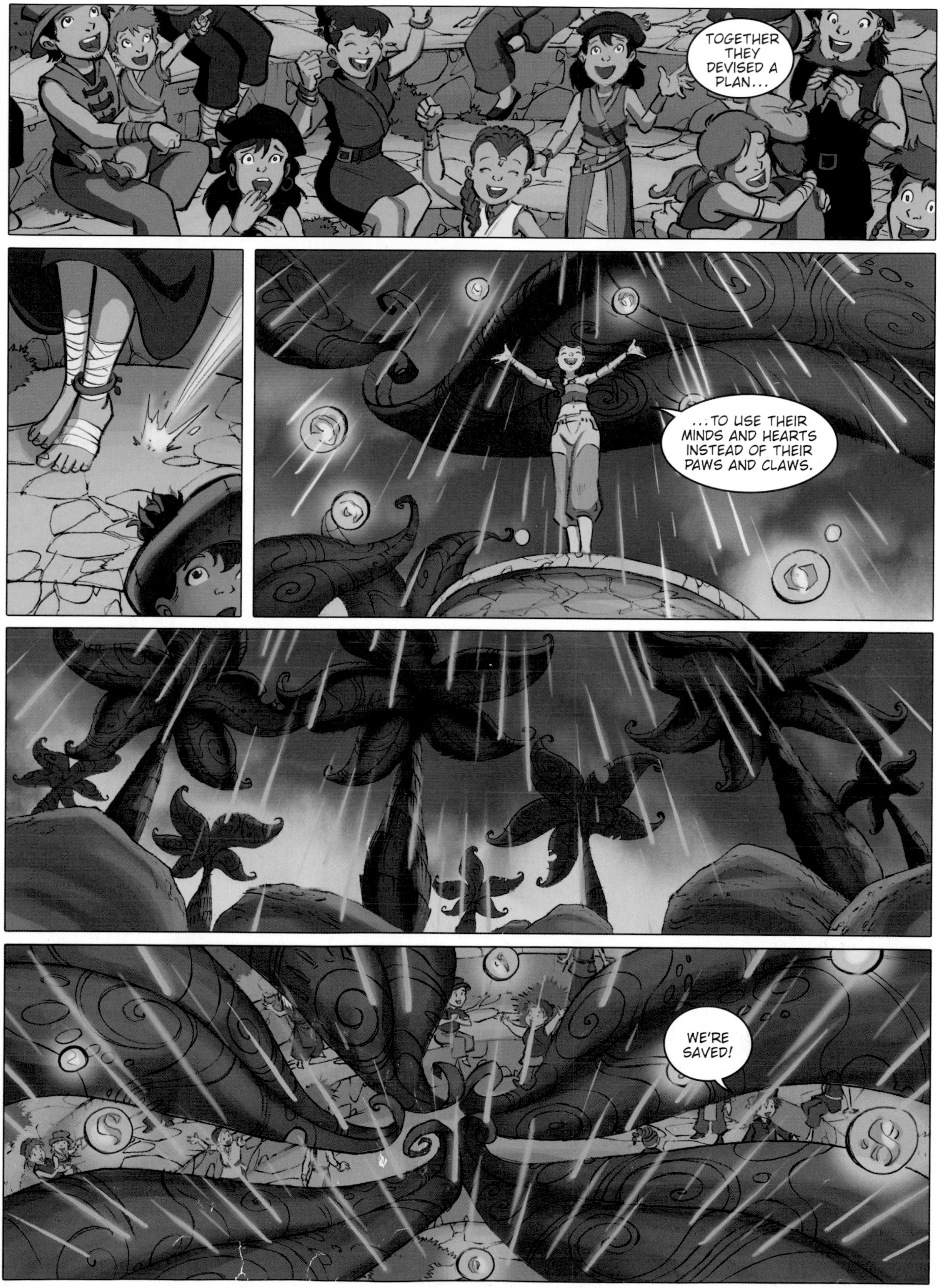

TOGETHER THEY DEVISED A PLAN...
...TO USE THEIR MINDS AND HEARTS INSTEAD OF THEIR PAWS AND CLAWS.
WE'RE SAVED!

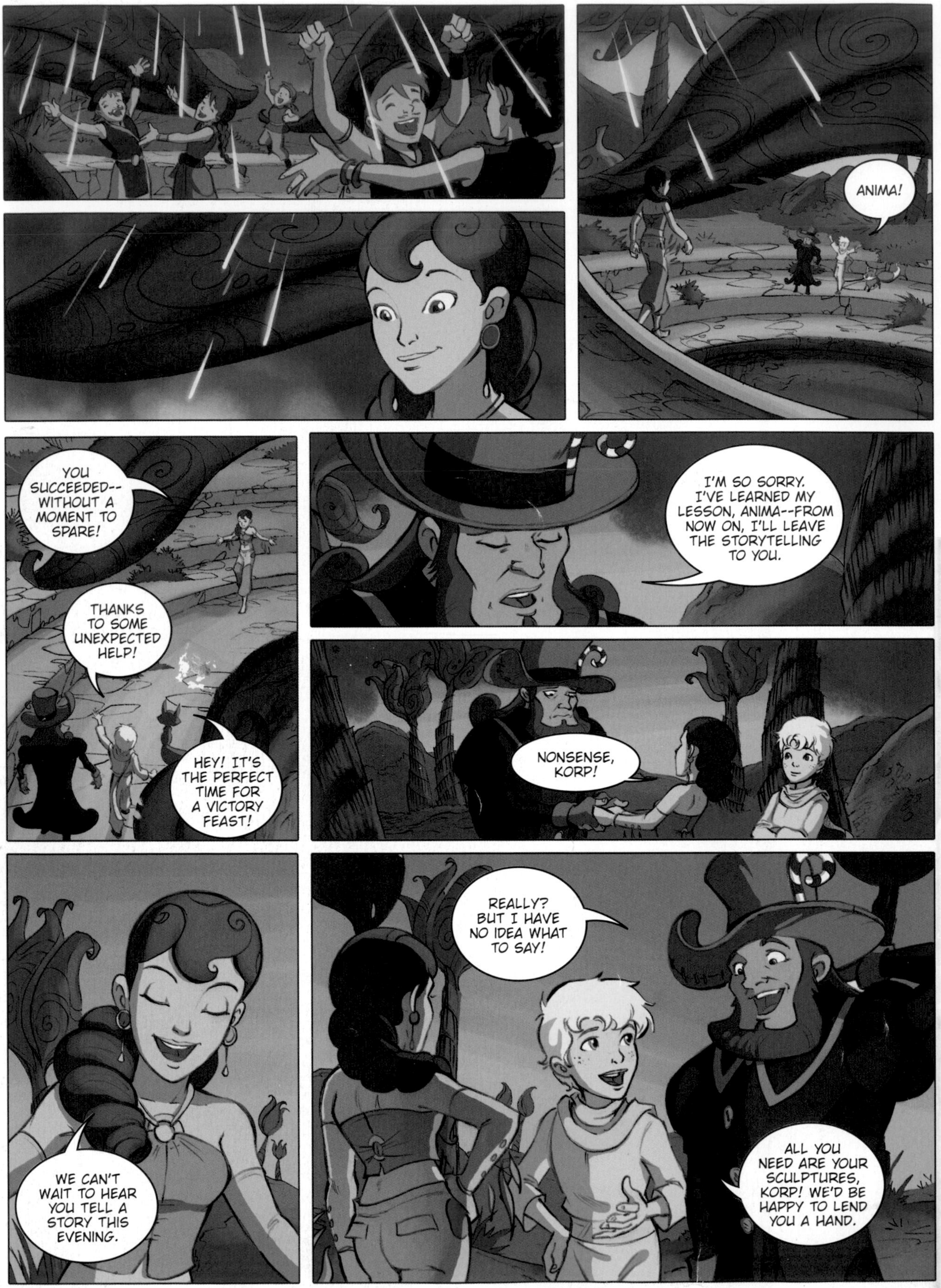
ANIMA!
YOU SUCCEEDED--WITHOUT A MOMENT TO SPARE!
THANKS TO SOME UNEXPECTED HELP!
HEY! IT'S THE PERFECT TIME FOR A VICTORY FEAST!
I'M SO SORRY. I'VE LEARNED MY LESSON, ANIMA--FROM NOW ON, I'LL LEAVE THE STORYTELLING TO YOU.
NONSENSE, KORP!
WE CAN'T WAIT TO HEAR YOU TELL A STORY THIS EVENING.
REALLY? BUT I HAVE NO IDEA WHAT TO SAY!
ALL YOU NEED ARE YOUR SCULPTURES, KORP! WE'D BE HAPPY TO LEND YOU A HAND.

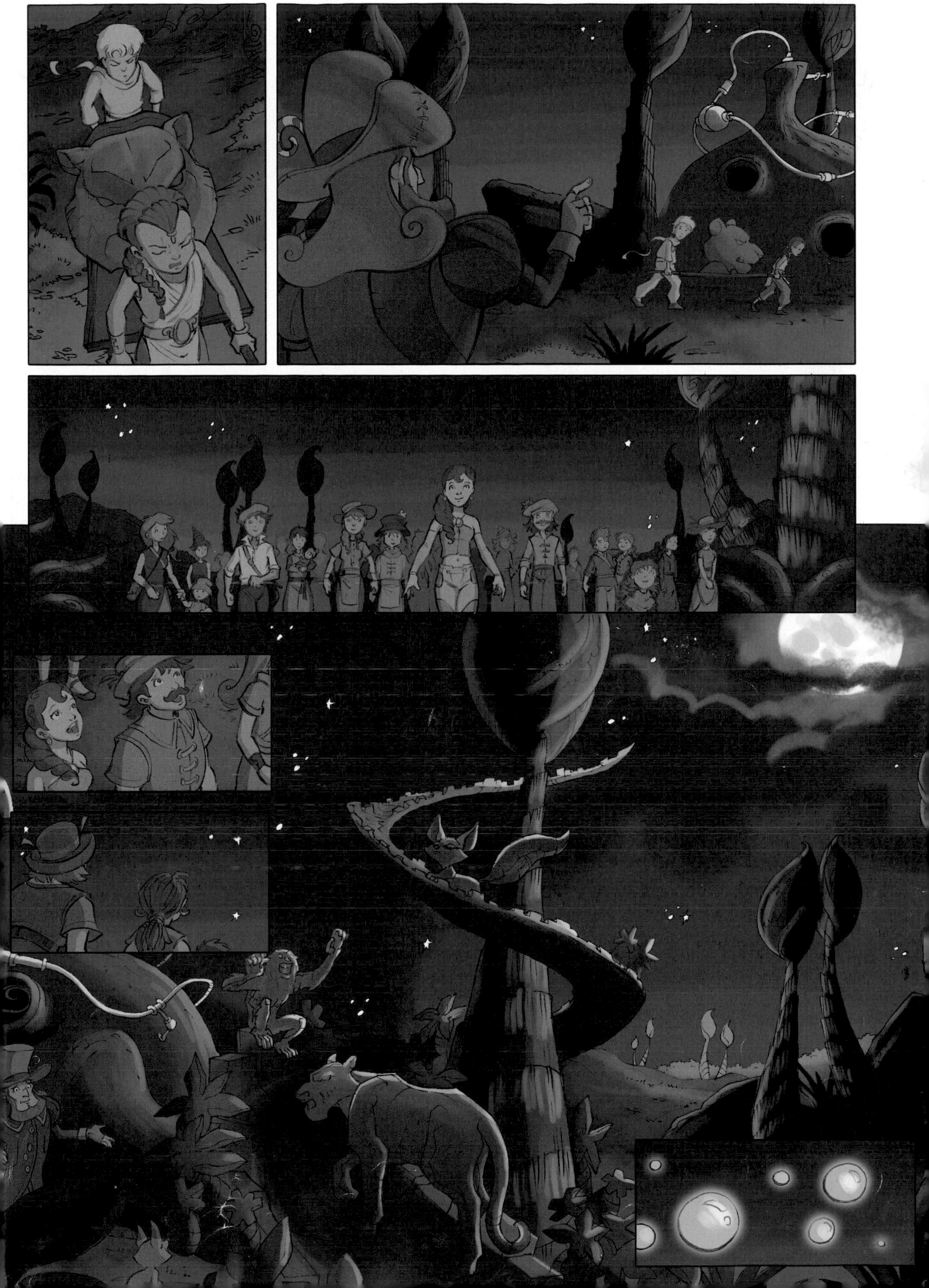

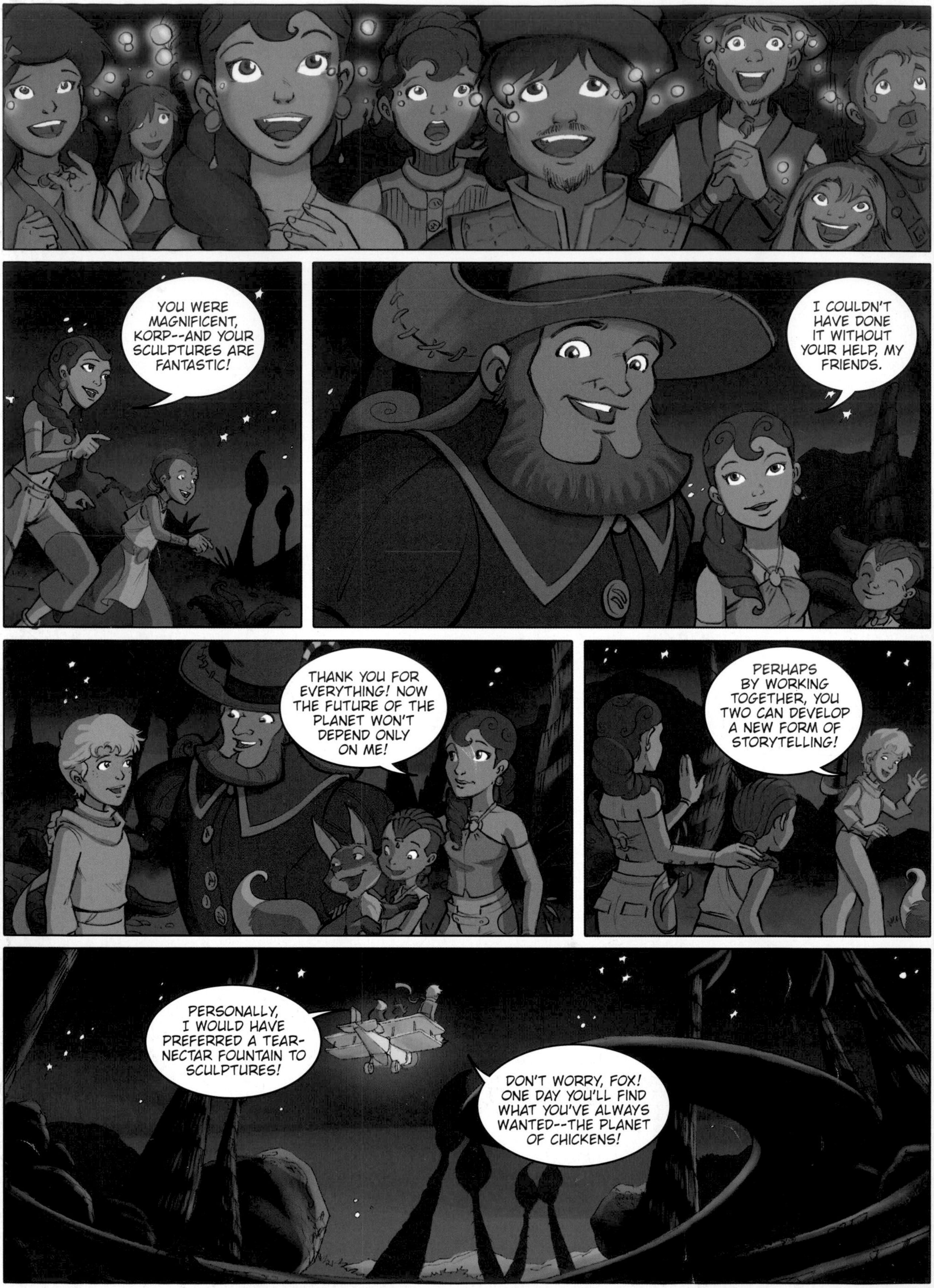
YOU WERE MAGNIFICENT, KORP--AND YOUR SCULPTURES ARE FANTASTIC!
I COULDN'T HAVE DONE IT WITHOUT YOUR HELP, MY FRIENDS.
THANK YOU FOR EVERYTHING! NOW THE FUTURE OF THE PLANET WON'T DEPEND ONLY ON ME!
PERHAPS BY WORKING TOGETHER, YOU TWO CAN DEVELOP A NEW FORM OF STORYTELLING!
PERSONALLY, I WOULD HAVE PREFERRED A TEAR-NECTAR FOUNTAIN TO SCULPTURES!
DON'T WORRY, FOX! ONE DAY YOU'LL FIND WHAT YOU'VE ALWAYS WANTED--THE PLANET OF CHICKENS!

THE END

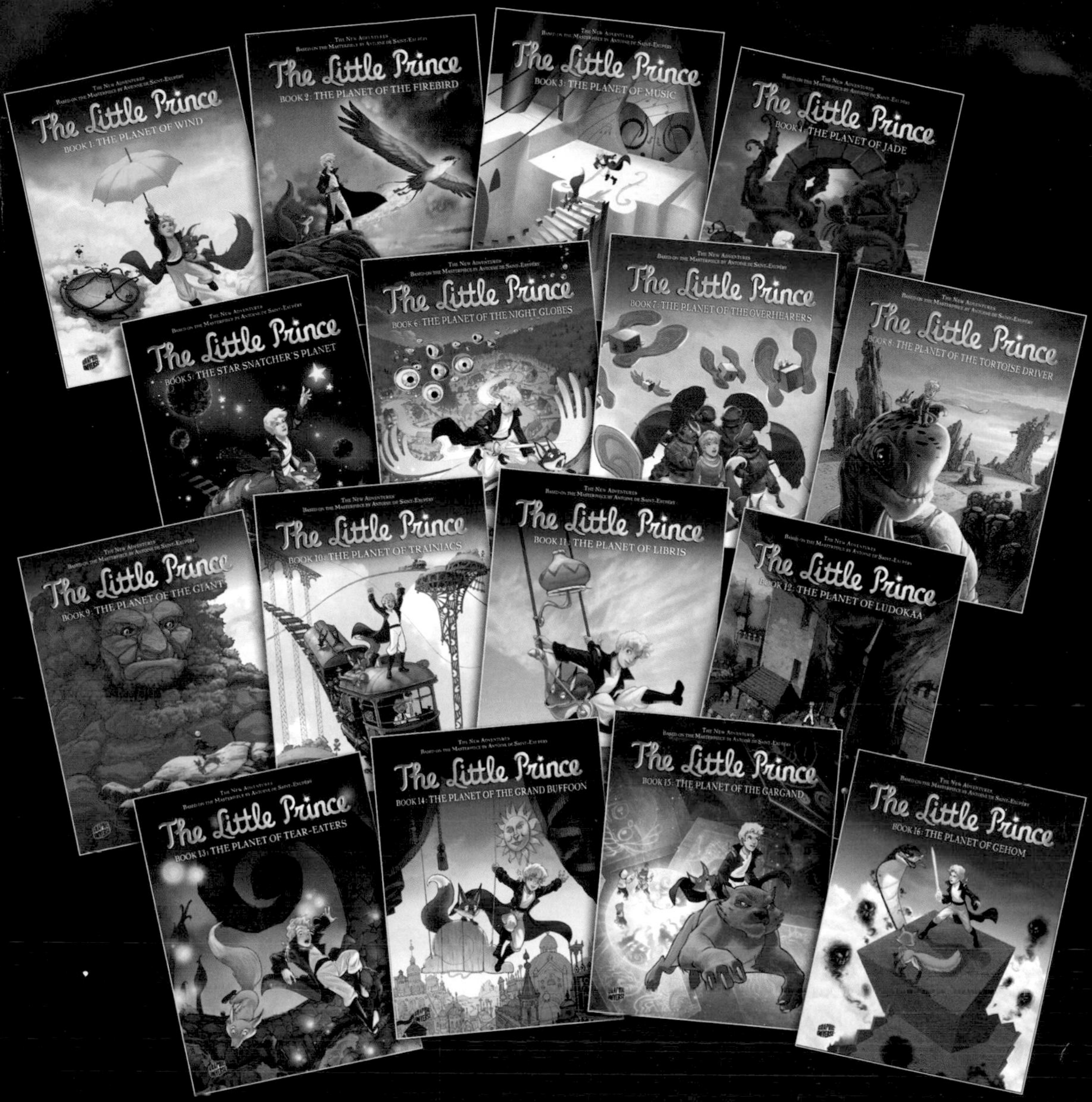
The Little Prince
BOOK 1: THE PLANET OF WIND
The Little Prince
BOOK 2: THE PLANET OF THE FIREBIRD
The Little Prince
BOOK 3: THE PLANET OF MUSIC
The Little Prince
THE PLANET OF JADE
The Little Prince
BOOK 5: THE STAR SNATCHER'S PLANET
The Little Prince
BOOK 6: THE PLANET OF THE NIGHT GLOBES
The Little Prince
BOOK 7: THE PLANET OF THE OVERHEARERS
The Little Prince
BOOK 8: THE PLANET OF THE TORTOISE DRIVER
The Little Prince
BOOK 9: THE PLANET OF THE GIANT
The Little Prince
BOOK 10: THE PLANET OF TRAINIACS
The Little Prince
BOOK 11: THE PLANET OF LIBRIS
The Little Prince
BOOK 12: THE PLANET OF LUDOKAA
The Little Prince
BOOK 13: THE PLANET OF TEAR-EATERS
The Little Prince
BOOK 14: THE PLANET OF THE GRAND BUFFOON
The Little Prince
BOOK 15: THE PLANET OF THE GARGAND
The Little Prince
BOOK 16: THE PLANET OF GEHOM

Book 1: The Planet of Wind

Book 2: The Planet of the Firebird

Book 3: The Planet of Music

Book 4: The Planet of Jade

Book 5: The Star Snatcher's Planet

Book 6: The Planet of the Night Globes

Book 7: The Planet of the Overhearers

Book 8: The Planet of the Tortoise Driver

Book 9 : The Planet of the Giant

Book 10 : The Planet of Trainiacs

Book 11 : The Planet of Libris

Book 12 : The Planet of Ludokaa

Book 13 : The Planet of Tear-Eaters

Book 14 : The Planet of the Grand Buffoon

Book 15 : The Planet of the Gargand

Book 16 : The Planet of Gehom

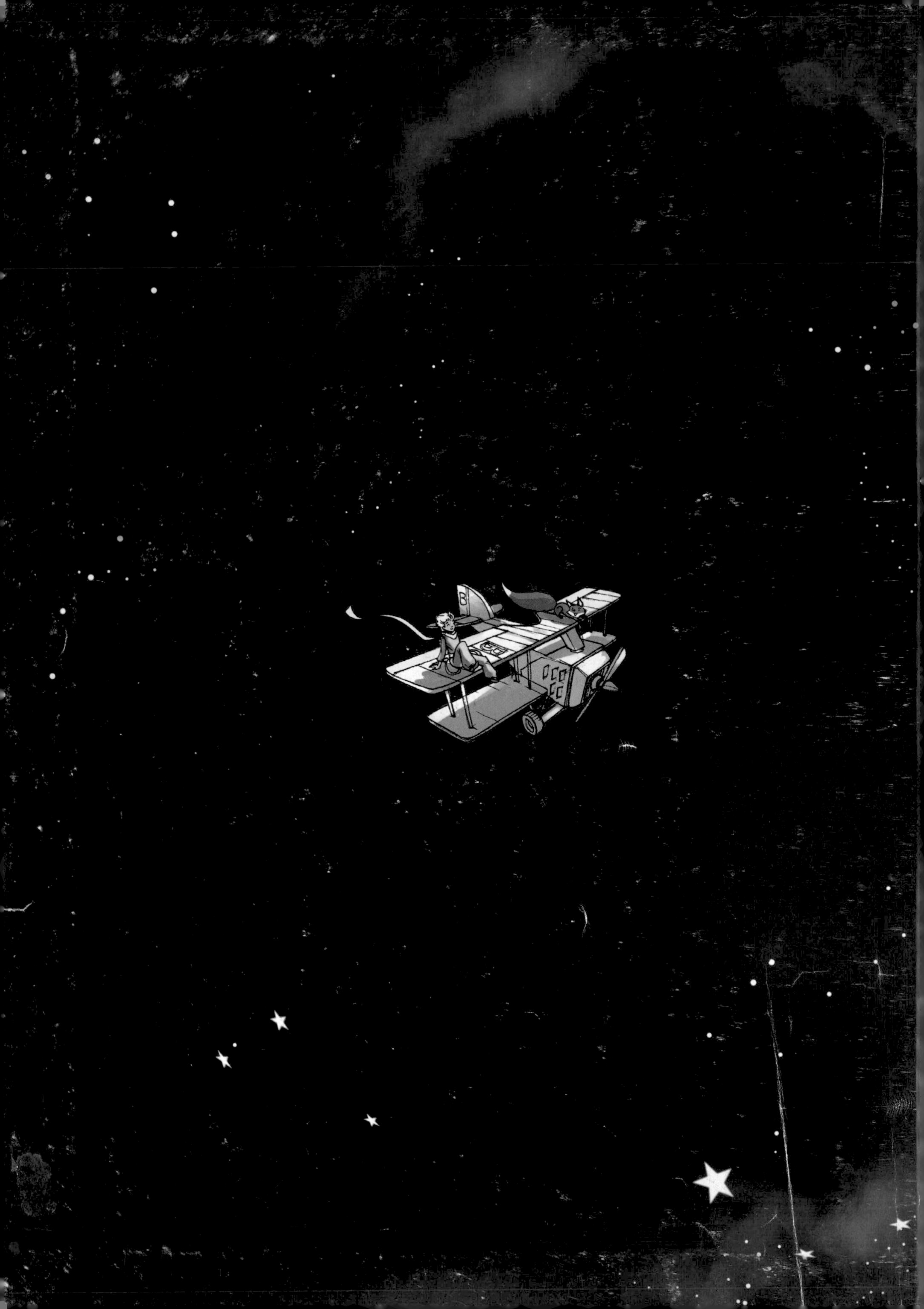